Was a Time When

A Novel That Asks,

"What Happens WHEN, Not IF, Resource Depletion,
Population Pressures, and Climate Change Push
The World of Our Grandchildren Into a Great Collapse?"

SAM PENNY

TwoPenny Publications

ISBN-10: 0975567136
ISBN-13: 9780975567135

Published by TwoPenny Publications
205 Rainbow Dr #10503
Livingston, TX 77399-2005

www.WasATimeWhen.com
TwoPennyPubs@WasATimeWhen.com

Printed in the United States of America

Front and Back cover photography courtesy of NASA

To Deborah Penny and Paula Gallegos
My two daughters who helped with the direction
and editing of this book

CONTENTS

PREFACE

I began this book in 2006 after watching the failure of the federal government and local authorities to handle the catastrophe produced by Hurricanes Katrina and Rita. I had been writing a third book in the *7.9 Scenario* series about the attempted recovery in Memphis from a major earthquake. I realized I could not publish my third book without being accused of plagiarizing the New Orleans *Times-Picayune* newspaper with my descriptions of how poorly the authorities would handle recovery after a major disaster.

My epiphany occurred when I realized that when world events really go bad, those in control most often can be expected to fail. I began to question why I saw so little response and preparations for the impending problems with resource depletion and climate change. Then when I saw how unwilling the establishment was to affect changes in the economic structure, even when faced with an awful mess with the banks and bankers, I realized that as things grew worse, the authorities were most likely going to hope that things would get better and just do nothing.

Since that time I watched a bubble of housing and debt overcome the world, while so many of the great managers kept saying everything would be okay. In the end, they just never seemed to understand how badly our society and culture had built a cage around itself.

My game is building scenarios, so I began to build a scenario of what could be expected in the remainder of this century. I used the projections of the doomers and the arguments of the saviors to try to understand what the world would be like.

In 2007 I hit upon the idea of telling the story through the eyes of someone who lived through the upcoming history. I began to construct a timeline for when things might happen and what the effects would be. I introduced descendants from the future as a means for finding something good about what might happen. In the end, I wrote the memoirs of an eighty-five-year-old man named Sam Hardy and a short story of a group from AD 3,100 searching for the source of their tribe.

My introduction of the genetic traits of red hair and a tail is purely for the purpose of differentiation. The key genetic trait for success in the future will be the ability to think rationally.

My novel is only one of the many possible scenarios for the future. I offer this tale as a cautionary work to explain to the present generations that the future is for them to determine. And if they do not get busy and point humanity in the right direction, their grandchildren will be swept up in the disasters that make up *Was a Time When*.

Sam Penny
December 2011

PROLOGUE: MAE 5, 3100

CosandJo completed his morning meditations and repeated his litany by rote from the *Book of J* as he traced the obligatory letter J on the palm of his hand.

Civilization died as it lost the knowledge and tools to make itself work.

People in all the lands starved, the weakest first, then the strong. New diseases followed close behind.

Chaos enveloped all the humans of the world, and the starving, diseased hordes fought amongst themselves and overran the lands.

For a while the elite survived, though not for long.

A few others evolved the talents and immunities to adapt to the new world. They came to be called Neu-humans. They are us, and we are the next species of the human race.

CosandJo opened his eyes and pushed a lock of red hair from his face. He murmured a supplemental prayer, "May my mind be clear, and my life lived with purpose," then added, "and may I find a sign of our ancestors, the roots of our tribe." He glanced over his shoulder, knowing he should not pray for specific results, but his wish seemed so broad that he did not think the forces controlling the universe would mind.

Squaring his shoulders, he scanned the bare earthen hummock. In several places pebbles lay exposed from the heavy rains that washed away the burned blackberry bushes covering the hill. He could see evidence of human activity from a thousand years past. The mound's shape affirmed its origin as a structure. He saw scattered shards of building materials from past structures on the surface, and nearby debris piles marked this area as part of a village. A prickly feeling ran from the nape of his neck to the stub of his tail, telling him that he must be close to the source of his tribe's roots. The fourteen-year-old apprentice archeologist pulled the mock-vellum sheet from the tube on his back, unrolled it, and studied the hand-drawn lines he had copied from the old deerskin map. He measured the distance by eye to the old creek bed, the direction to the hillock to the south, and to the valley notch to the east. CosandJo's comparison of the map to local landmarks convinced him that he must be standing at the very entrance to The Old Man's Home as told in the *Book of J*, his tribe's legendary record.

After the seas killed his son and threatened his tribe, The Old Man led the tribe to their new home in Suter Land and built his home on the hill above the creek. There he lived with his tribesmen until they all died.

CosandJo poked into the mound of dry sand and gravel, and he heard the metal point of his digging stick clank against a solid object with a resonant sound different from that of ordinary lava rock. He reached down to brush the clods aside and exposed a smooth, green surface. He knelt to push more dirt and sand away, uncovering what looked like the corner of a green-stone box. Digging around the object with his fingers, he loosened it from the surrounding clay and lifted a tiny casket from its crypt.

Placing the box on the ground, he stared at the treasure, wondering. What could be the contents of a chest such as this from The Old Man's Home? Convention required that he race back without delay to his faculty mentor, ProfSir ElderJan, but his curiosity overcame that inferred command. Fascinated, he wiped away the encrusted dirt from the side of the box.

CosandJo's sensitive fingers felt a crease. He traced the groove all the way around the chest. Lifting the box into his left palm, his right hand grasped the top and twisted. His freckled face colored a deep red as the top of the box spun. Recognizing that it must be a lid, he rotated the top counter-clockwise several times to loosen it. Then he lifted the stone cover to reveal a cylindrical hollow, and inside he could see several molded silicon oxide disks like those exhibited in the university museum. Storage Disks, the ProfSirs called them, storage for the knowledge gathered in the ancient times by the Old World before the Great Collapse.

Now he could wait no longer. Replacing the lid and wrapping the box in his shroud, he ran to his three-wheeled cycle. He placed the package in the front carrier and peddled as hard as he could over the dirt field back to the big crushed rock corridor that led to the encampment four klicks south. He had to show his prize to his leader ProfSir ElderJan and to his fellow students on the archeological expedition. His finding would help them explore the remains of the civilization that lived here a thousand years before, and more than that, he had assuredly found solid evidence for the roots of his tribe.

Chapter 1: Memoirs

May 10, 2099

ProfSir ElderJan, a red-haired man of fifty-five, accepted the green box from CosandJo. The breathless lad exclaimed, "Sir, I just returned from my scouting trip to Suter Land, and I found this box in a mound that I identified as The Old Man's Home, just where the *Book of J* said it would be. I believe this is an actual artifact from the home of The Old Man and relates to the roots of our tribe.

ElderJan stroked the green stone chest, noting that CosandJo must have already opened it. He frowned at the young boy. "What you bring is good, CosandJo, but you know you must not be so impulsive as to open such a treasure without your elders present."

ElderJan smiled as CosandJo bowed his head, held up his hands to protect his ears, and mumbled, "Noted, Sir." No knuckle clout would be needed this time.

Six months earlier, ProfSir ElderJan, chair of the Neo-Archeology Department at the University of Hudson Bay, stood before his peers in the Chamber of Profs and pleaded, "As my contribution to our Millennium Celebration, I petition this body to fund an archeological expedition to the Lands of Oregon for the purpose of collecting scientific information and artifacts from the time of the Great Collapse."

The Dean of Profs asked, "What good do you expect to come from this expedition?"

"We should be able to recover even more of the science records of the original humans, and this work could provide a better understanding of the origins of our species.

Another Prof asked, "Why do you persist in studying those humans who came before us? We know they understood little. Their technology was great, but there is little from the past that is of use to us. We must live with what we have."

ElderJan replied, "We have already lost so much of the knowledge that they developed over their two-hundred-year industrial revolution. The more we can save, the easier it will be for our civilization."

The Dean continued, "Who would be on this expedition, and what would be your schedule?"

"I will take three of my staff and my thirteen apprentices on the expedition so they can learn firsthand the technologies and science of archeology and the practices of good salvage. We will leave next April when the coastal rains begin to wane, and will return by August before the dust storms set in."

The antagonist continued his assault. "Those that came before us were so wrong. There cannot be value in studying their mistakes."

ElderJan drew in a deep breath and explained as he had so many times in the past. "The civilization of a thousand years ago achieved the epitome of technical development for the human race. Their accomplishments were so far beyond what we can hope for today, they seem like magic to us now. And yet, the entire world failed, and the human race almost became extinct. I believe we must understand what they had, and why they failed. If we do not, we can suffer the same fate as our ancestors."

The Dean calmed the discussion. "Yes, I agree we need to understand our past and identify the mistakes that were made back then. This is a worthy effort."

After a brief discussion, the assembly voted to approve the expedition with one dissension. ElderJan said, "Thank you, I am sure we will bring back at least one treasure of great importance to our tribe, and you will all agree the it was worth the time and effort." He turned and hurried away to begin preparations for the trip.

ElderJan carefully took the uppermost silicon disc from the box and turned it over to look at both sides. "There appears to be no damage. It looks pristine, but most of these old disks are etched with signals our tools cannot decode."

CosandJo leaned over the old man's shoulder for a better view. "But can the code on this one be read by the Magic Reader?" he asked, pointing to the strange-looking machine on the bench nearby.

The ProfSir's Magic Reader was one of four such devices found ten years earlier in a storage bunker near the Calgary site south of the university. Techs at the university learned that when connected to one of the Magic Puters that had been found decades before, the Reader could decipher the signals on the storage disks and send them to the Puter to be spoken to the operator.

These ancient devices were remains from a civilization that had thrived a thousand years ago, and they incorporated the advanced features of Artificial Intelligence and Compact Storage Discs. But the technologists of the thirty-first century could not figure out how they did it.

"We can only try." ElderJan placed the first disk from the box into the rotator of the Magic Reader. He began to spin the plate under the Magic Reader to help the reader suck signals from the disk and send them to the Puter.

After a moment the Puter spoke in a metallic voice, "Scanning first file. Format is Word Doc. Language is Aenglish. Contents can be translated."

CosandJo jumped with joy. "ProfSir, I found this box in Suter Land at The Old Man's Home according to my copies of the ancient maps, so this disk must tell us of where our tribe came from."

"Perhaps. Perhaps. But we must hear what the disk says to know for sure. The whole class must listen to what it tells us. Call them together here while I preview the other files on this disk."

The University of Hudson Bay, recognized as the source of the Neu-human population on the Northern Continent, displayed records in its museum supporting the claim that its founders created the school during the Great Collapse of the twenty-first century, over a thousand years before.

Early in the twenty-second century, the population of the enclave dropped to near-extinction levels. Over time, by employing all the survival practices its leaders could muster, the small band recovered and grew. After a thousand years, descendants of those original pio-neers spread back across the upper reaches of the Northern Conti-nent.

The tribe's close brush with total extermination selected their domi-nant genetic traits, and those who survived passed those character-istics to those who made it through the genetic bottle-neck. Their wispy red har and short, hair-covered tails were the most obvious physical markers, but their amazing mental capabilities—a photographic memory and an inherent ability to understand and act upon reality in a rational manner—forged the primary character of the new race. They called themselves the Neu-humans in recognition of their distinct genetic advance over the original human race.

Remnants of the original species of humans who populated the land prior to the Great Collapse still roamed the dry deserts to the south, surviving as best they could as hunter/gatherers. They lived as savages and no longer represented any threat to the civilization to the north. Their species could never again control the earth.

When all his students sat before him, ProfSir ElderJan approached his pillows, sat cross-legged on them before his budding archeologists, and smiled his all-knowing best. He watched as CosandJo squirmed at the front of the group on his horse hair rug, legs crossed in the style proper for an apprentice to receive instruction. Cool air from the fog blowing up the Umpqua River canyon filtered into the big headquarters tent and around the gathering.

ElderJan spoke in a deep, heavy voice. "Class, our school specializes in the study of the original human race and their science and the beginnings of the Neu-humans. We have collected a variety of artifacts from the ancient times and added them to the museum for study by you and our future students. Our trip from the north and over the Cascadia Mountains to the banks of this river has already proven to be a huge success."

Pointing to CosandJo, the teacher showed his pride and beamed in a broad smile. "My first nephew, a student and your compatriot, CosandJo, discovered a stone box of ancient storage disks in Suter Land, four klicks north of here. He located the archeological site after much research, reading from the *Book of J* and studying the old maps handed down from ancient times. You must make yourselves like him to be of value to our Neu-human civilization. I am proud of my apprentice."

A small wave of grunts sounded in applause, and CosandJo blushed and shrugged, obviously pleased to be acknowledged. ProfSir Elder-Jan rarely complimented any of his students, even those of his own family.

The ProfSir cleared his throat to quiet the class and prevent any excessive displays of exuberance. He continued, "Today we shall listen to an ancient recording of one man's experiences during the Great Collapse. His name was Sam Hardy, and he experienced the events that led to the collapse of the society that preceded the birth of our Neuhuman civilization."

His class watched with rapt attention as he turned to the black box on the table and said the voice-command, "Puter, please translate and say Doc File Chap-1 from the Sam disk."

A metallic voice came from the Puter box. "Translating from Aenglish. Hold."

The Puter paused for a moment, and when it spoke again, it was in the husky, accented tone of an old man.

My name is Sam Hardy. Today I am beginning to write the memoirs of my life. I am composing my story on an old laptop computer that my friend George resurrected two years ago. All of my running electronics agree that today is Sunday, May 10, 2099, nearly twenty-one centuries since the birth of Jesus Christ—to some a prophet, to others a savior. I am agnostic and take no position on that matter.

I shall call my writings, "Was a Time When: The Story of Samuel Julian Hardy." The length of my memoirs and how much I tell depends upon how much I remember, how long I live, and how long the mood stays with me. I chose as my audience those ghosts from the past who could not understand the events happening around them.

In times past I never thought about writing down current events, but I remember when things were so much different than now. Now I am the last person in this village, the last of my tribe. It is possible that I am even the last of civilization in these parts, for I have not seen anyone for two months, except for Ralph. And now he's dead. Writing it all down just seems like the thing to do now.

People always called me Sam. I turned eighty-four last March. I live amidst the remains of an old RV park near Sutherlin in Oregon. For those of you in the future, RV means "recreational vehicle." It is a movable house with wheels and a built in fossil-fuel engine. Back when one could find a supply of liquid fuel to run the engine, people followed the good weather and moved their RVs from place to place. When the fuel ran out, each RV stopped in its tracks and transformed into a wretched hut on a steel foundation with useless wheels.

Pioneers founded the town of Sutherlin in the 1880s as a lumber camp in the foothills of the Cascade Mountains, not far from the North Fork of the Umpqua River. After the lumber industry died, it became a community where older people came to retire and live, many of them in RVs.

This RV park, what's left of it anyway, is a small group of stationary wrecks next to Cooper Creek that runs down from where the old town reservoir used to be. Ralph, George, and I scavenged through all the old RVs and collected solar panels, wire, batteries, and pieces of electronics. George resurrected this old computer and found a cache of ultraDVDs, the kind that keep their data for more than a hundred years. Ralph even found one of those special pseudo-stone storage boxes for DVDs, the kind that extends their life even more. I can store a DVD backup of my memoirs in that box, so my records will outlast the environment, no matter how hot or wet it gets. This place is a scavenger's treasure chest.

Everyone who lived in this day and age did salvage. One of the reasons my tribe picked Sutherlin was its salvage potential.

Whatever we found we turned into something useful and operational to aid our survival. George helped me rebuild a hand-powered shortwave radio. That radio let my tribe hear multiband broadcasts, the few left to hear, from all over the globe. All other means of telecommunications failed. We never found a transmitter that worked, but our meager supply of electrical power could not send a strong enough signal anyway.

I am now alone. Ralph Myers killed himself last week. At least with him gone there is more for me to eat. Very little grows around here anymore—no rain. I can find a few dried acorns and roots. Unless I find another cache of food, I figure by this next fall I'll be a victim of the starvation that killed so many here and around the world.

My personal comforts are pretty well taken care of. The weather keeps getting hotter, but so far it is bearable. If the old projections are right, this Oregon weather is the same as the weather they experienced inland from the coast of Baja California in Mexico a century ago.

Things are going pretty well for me on the electrical front with three functioning solar panels, though they don't produce power like they used to. George found some long-life nickel-iron batteries in the scrap heap, and they still hold a good charge. There is sufficient power to run the computer during the day and LED lights at night so I can operate the short-wave radio into the evening.

There is still some amount of civilization in other places, but it is falling there as well as here. I hear about it on the shortwave radio, but I am receiving less and less news every day. It's a combination of little real news to report and censorship on what news is reported. Once in a while I pick up transmissions from overseas. I wish I could understand all the languages my first wife, Abby, knew. For the most part, the NAF—that's the North American Federation—controls what people hear, but there are enough outlaw transmissions to fill in the missing details.

For instance, there's this fellow on the radio who calls himself Job. He seems to think he's a reincarnation from the Holy Bible. Job broadcasts on Wednesday evenings, and last week he said, "The world's population in 2099 is down to six hundred million people. God is getting even."

I did a quick calculation and concluded that at least seven billion people died in the last sixty years from global pandemics, the nuclear wars, and starvation. The loss of food and water in so much of the world led to total chaos with riots, ethnic cleansing, and other forms of barbarism. I wonder at times what God is so pissed about.

The Military Forces of the NAF pretty much run the country from the Arctic Ocean to Central America. The NAF is strongest along the West Coast and in the Southeast. Middle America is semi-independent. It's a lack of transportation issue. Without liquid fuels, airplanes don't fly much and troop transports don't get very far. That leaves control to the foot soldiers and horse cavalry. It's a big country and on foot they can't keep up with it all. Along the coast it's much easier, and Navy and Coast Guard units are in command. Wind keeps the sailboats moving.

Last night on the radio a NAF reporter stated, "It is now six degrees centigrade warmer in the temperate zone than two hundred years ago." For those from long ago, that's nine degrees Fahrenheit. "A lot of heating has taken place in the Amazon basin and equatorial Pacific where temperatures climbed more than eight degrees centigrade. The Arctic heated even more, and sea ice is gone even in winter, as are most of the ice fields of Greenland. The rapid melt of ice in Antarctica caused sea levels to rise 2.7 meters so far."

The reporter said scientists admit this is much more than the rise expected even thirty years ago and way beyond the official predictions published in 2008. He went on to say that some estimate that sea levels could rise another fifteen meters in the next couple of centuries. I still don't think they are telling us how bad it will be, but at least the authorities are admitting there may be a problem.

Higher temperatures and changing water patterns around the world have created drought and turned long-time farmlands into deserts. Hardest hit are Australia, China, India, middle Africa, parts of the Russian steppes, southern South America, and America's Midwest. Water wells in the planet's most productive farmlands are dry, and there is never enough runoff into the rivers to make a difference. But the NAF reporter encouraged us. "However, folks, some people are saying that farming is a growing industry near the Arctic Circle. You might consider applying for a migration permit at your local Army Recruiter's office." Sure, I said, give me a migration permit, but does that come with a train ticket?

Some say the best place in this country's temperate zone is the southeastern states, except for Florida, most of which is underwater now. Job says the southeast must be prime country. "Atlanta is the seat of power for the North American Federation's military. The generals think they're the rulers of the country and their troops use most of our remaining fossil fuels." Job sounds belligerent.

I've listened to other individual radio operators on the short-wave bands around the country. It's a good way to keep up on things. Harry in St. Jo, Missouri, reports the Midwest from the Rockies to the Appalachians is so dry that most farmlands are uninhabitable. Only settlements sitting near a large lake or beside a river have any future. There isn't enough rain to keep things growing. There's still a lot of electric power generation from coal in Illinois, but the water shortage in the Ohio valley is severe. Water levels in the Great Lakes fell two hundred feet, but the drop stabilized when people quit drawing so much water out of them.

Tom in Dayton, Ohio, says people are trying to grow food in what he called "wet-veggie-beds" because they keep the humidity so high. These are plastic sheet-covered houses, but there is a severe shortage of plastics feedstock, and that makes building the wet-veggie-beds a problem. They're still using petro and natgas for transportation. You'd think they would learn to ride a horse or walk.

A few short-wave radio reports come from the northeast U.S.. The conditions there sound horrendous. I remember how Barney in New Jersey reported the warming, flooding, disease, and starvation to be far worse than he ever expected. The biggest problem in the northeast is their high population density; people had nowhere to go to escape the hurricanes and pandemics. When food supplies ran out almost overnight six years ago, a total collapse of society struck Barney's area, and he signed off for good.

Southern California, Nevada, Arizona, and western Mexico returned to a dry desert, infused with scattered bits of human debris. J Macius says most of the old houses and apartments around Phoenix have been salvaged, and little is left but the foundations and slabs.

Disruption of water supplies to southern California from the Colorado River and the Sierra Nevada Mountains forced the mass migration from the Tijuana, San Diego, and Los Angeles basins to the north. That transplanted the gangster society into central California. Deb said on the radio that towns around the San Francisco Bay and Sacramento Sea got along okay for a time, but gangs now control the whole area. As the food supplies ran out, the collapse of society created the savage hordes my tribe fought for so many years.

Several radio operators report that Alaska, Yukon, and the Northwest Territory are looking good at this time. Climate warming is making them more hospitable, and the area didn't start with a whole lot of extra people there to begin with. Of course, the migrations from Mexico and the U.S. states are starting to fill much of the northern area near the Arctic Circle.

Job talked again last night about bad things yet to come. He said, "Climate and lack of food will get worse in the coming years. The NAF's population could drop to fifty million by 2125." If Job keeps spouting off like that over the radio, the NAF Military and CIA Forces are going to find him and shut him down for good.

As long as I can remember, the government never liked people who said negative things about the world. It reflected on how well the government was doing.

ProfSir ElderJan said, "Puter, please pause. Class, think of what you heard so far. What information is new to us?"

CosandJo said, "Sam Hardy's description of the state of the world is pretty bleak, but it sounds like water made the biggest difference back in those times. With water the population might farm and survive, but without it, nothing could survive."

ElderJan replied, "Yes, water made a big difference. Some studies suggest that water became more important than energy. Of course, the old civilization did not understand how to pump water without a big energy resource. Also, note that Sam says the name of his home is Sutherlin, not Suter Land as we call it. From this time on we will use its original name."

SamJan, another student, asked, "ProfSir, Sam talks about a sea level rise of 2.7 meters with another fifteen meters expected. I learned in my meteorology class last year that sea levels stopped rising several centuries ago. How much rise happened since Sam's time?"

"Estimates are that the sea level rose twenty-two meters in seven centuries from its level just before the Great Collapse. It stabilized about three centuries ago. So it had just begun to rise in Sam's time."

One of the first year apprentices asked, "It sounds like lots of people used radio. Did radio work like what we have now?"

"MeJe, there was very little radio activity when Sam wrote this chapter, but at one time before the Great Collapse, the number of radios in the world exceeded the number of people. Civilization mastered the science of micro-electronics and used that science in many, many devices, including radios with images. The computer Sam used to write his memoirs resulted from the same science. Our Puter and Magic Reader are based upon that science. But today, micro-electronics are quite rare because the science and technology to make them has either been lost, or the materials required to make them are no longer available. We must rely on whatever remains we can salvage of that old technology."

"Oh, it must have been nice back then."

ElderJan smiled and said, "Yes, and you will study about these devices in next year's classes. But let us continue. Puter, please resume."

The metallic voice spoke again, "Continuing Doc File Chap-1 from Sam."

///////// \\\\\\\\\

I suppose some would consider me to be one of the luckier ones of our tribe; I am one who survived the last sickness. Or maybe I am the unlucky one. Now that Ralph is gone, all I can do is slowly starve and die alone. Loneliness is not good. I'm not ready to take Ralph's easy way out—but I might change my mind if things get much worse.

Ralph sealed the fate of my tribe here at Sutherlin when he let that outlander come into the village back in November. A big storm tore through the area, and Ralph got to feeling sorry for this guy walking north along the old Interstate 5 roadway. Ralph whined to me, "Honestly, Sam, I didn't know he was sick. Besides, it took him another two weeks to show any symptoms."

That happened seven months ago, and once started, the sickness spread throughout our little tribe in less than two weeks. Everyone became sick.

Two left the community, and twenty-six died. The three of us who survived that plague buried everyone else and cleaned up the place. We kept things tidy for a while. With only three to feed, our larder provided plenty of food. Then supplies began to run low, and we realized that trouble still surrounded us. No one bothered to tend the garden or fish or cure food or collect acorns, and we depleted our stores.

Four months ago, the first week in February, George slipped on an icy rock in Cooper Creek trying to chase down a salmon. He cut his leg something fierce, and it got infected. The leg swelled up and purple and green lines appeared under the skin until he died. Before dying he told me, "My flesh is filled with poison from the gangrene in my leg, so bury me deep and away from the creek." Ralph and I dragged brush over his grave so the coyotes wouldn't dig him up.

After that Ralph and I played checkers every day for hours on end. His cough sounded raspy and harsh, even worse when the winds picked up and blew the dust around. He kept telling me how bad he felt and how much he wanted his wife. I told him to shut up. Once I hit him over the head to make him quit. His whining got worse and worse, but at least his hoard of booze dried up, so he didn't get roaring drunk like in the past.

Wednesday morning I heard a loud blast and ran outside. There on the ground lay Ralph, bleeding from a hole in his head. Somewhere he found an old pistol and, standing in the path beside my house, shot himself. At last, his search for peace of mind proved successful.

It took some effort to bury Ralph's remains up the hill. I considered hanging him by his heels and butchering him like I used to do with a deer, but decided I had enough food and it was not worth the extra effort.

So now I am alone. I still live in an old RV shell that has been refurbished several times over. Most of the other structures around me are falling in decay, and the gardens have more weeds than useful plants. I can still find camas down in the flats. The creek is running enough water to fill my needs. The days are turning warmer and the clouds are going away. It is lonely here by myself with only the radio to listen.

When I consider my situation, the probability of my being at this place in this time must be near zero. So much happened to make it so. It took the actions of billions of people to create the world I live in. Some acted on purpose, some acted wrong, most just followed the herd. It took my perseverance in searching for safety for my tribe to drive me to this place. At least I acted on purpose.

But I should start at the beginning. That is what I will do in my next chapter. Maybe those of you who read this can then understand how I happened to be here today.

The Puter said, "End of File Chap-1. Should I continue to File Chap-2?"

ProfSir ElderJan stopped turning the rotator on the Magic Reader and massaged his arm. "Not now, Puter. Please pause and let my arm rest." He sensed the interest generated by the story in his young helpers, and he could use that enthusiasm.

"Remember, class, folklore says that our tribe originated from this region in the Lands of Oregon. But we are here to look for science from before the Great Collapse, and everyone must continue their fieldwork. We still must do much research and study before the summer dust storms force us back to Hudson Bay. The Puter tells me that there are fifteen more files on this disk describing conditions leading up to the year 2100. I will review these files, and after each day of hard work, we will listen to the next of the series in the order that Sam created them. In sixteen days' time, we will all know Sam's entire story."

CosandJo burst out, "And it will tell us of our roots. It will tell us from where we came and how we fit in the *Book of J*. It will tell..."

ElderJan interrupted. "It will tell us what happened in those ancient times. There is nothing in this disc to tell us anything about our roots. The *Book of J* is just a legend. Be quiet about roots. We must learn from their science."

"But..."

"Quiet. No roots."

Chapter 2: Sammy the Kid

March 15, 2015

CosandJo's impatience shivered through his body and tingled his tail. All day he and the rest of the class searched over the breadth of the hillside just north of the Umpqua River to identify likely digging spots. In several of the mounds they uncovered bits of concrete, aluminum, and rusted steel. Mixed in the debris, shards of fiberglass glistened from time to time.

They had wasted a whole day. They'd found nothing of scientific interest.

He had thought all day of how his class could listen to Sam's story as recorded on the Magic Disk, to learn about the beginnings of his tribe. He now sat in the front row as the class arranged their hairy rugs in a semicircle and waited. CosandJo reached behind to rub his tail to calm the quivering.

ProfSir ElderJan strode into the tent and stood beside his pillow. He tapped his leggings with his digging stick. "Good evening, class. You worked hard today, and that is good. You deserve a rest."

He sat down on the pillow. "Today we shall continue with Sam Hardy's memoirs. This next chapter tells of his birth and early years when he lived in a land of plenty, but a land with problems as it began to fall apart." The ProfSir looked over his class. "As we listen, contrast this part of Sam's story with your early life. What is different? What is the same?"

CosandJo masked his impatience for the reading to start. He could never understand why the ProfSir wanted to talk so much.

"Now there is more to hear," the ProfSir said. "Puter, please speak File Chap-2." He began to turn the crank round and round to rotate the disk under the reader head.

March 2015: that was the time when I officially entered the world. My birth certificate in Fresno, California, recorded my date of birth as March 15, 2015. Mom, on the other hand, claimed that her midwife "birthed me" at 11:58 p.m., two minutes before the Ides of March. Mom complained to anyone who would listen how "that woman took her own sweet time to look at the clock."

My dad, Tom, named me after two of my great-grandfathers: Samuel Hardy and Julian Boone. I became Samuel Julian Hardy, Sammy for short.

Mom and Dad never talked about their life and relationship before they conceived me, but they did get married after I came along. "Guess we wanted to be old-fashioned," Dad explained. He told me that when Mom got pregnant, they thought long and hard about having a baby, what with the instability and uncertain future of the world of 2014. He emphasized that they made sure I would be the last. "You're lucky to be alive," he said to me when I turned four. I have never forgotten nor forgiven him for pointing that out to me.

Two months after I joined the family, Dad and Mom had their formal ceremony, and Dad transferred in the California state government to Sacramento as a socioeconomic analyst. Our family moved to a one-bedroom apartment downtown so he could walk to work. Mom tutored her students in mathematics from home over the Internet. I just grew like a little pig with red hair and a stubby tail, the first indications of my mutations.

I proved to be smart from the start with a different way of understanding things. Mom said she knew she had produced a prodigy before I reached the age of one. I could gurgle words at seven months and spoke sentences by the end of my first year. I remember sitting in a highchair and throwing spoons of food at people around me because they wouldn't include me in their conversations. I told them how they didn't understand what they were talking about—they all needed to think straight. Of course, my language skills were not refined at that age so they didn't understand what I said.

On my first birthday, I told Mom, "Cake has one candle." She hugged me and said, "Your curly red hair, freckles, and that awful tail come from the Hardy side of the family, but I know you get your brains from the Boone side." She looked over, smiled big at Dad, gave me a peck on the cheek, and helped me blow out the candle on the cake.

Mom never understood the error in her logic. My brain contained a dominant Hardy mutation that showed up in me before the age of one, and years later I saw the same thought patterns and photographic memory in my cousin Marsha and her kids. It came from Dad's side of my family, along with the red hair and tail.

The ProfSir said, "Puter, pause for a moment. Class, we have just heard that Sammy had all the genetic traits of a Neu-human—exceptional mental powers, red hair, freckles, and a tail—and we now know these characteristics showed up as dominant traits in the Hardy family. This is a very important finding."

CosandJo smiled broadly and exclaimed, "I am right! Sam must have been The Old Man. I found our tribe's roots."

ElderJan barked impatiently, "CosandJo, you are speculating. It may be important, but it is not proof. Now be quiet." He calmed his voice and said, "Puter, continue."

In time I learned that the world had become a mess long before I came along. The Mikando oil-well blowout in 2010 had been bad enough. Then an economic depression enveloped the world when country after country could not cover the massive debts they had created for themselves, made possible by a central bank/fractional reserve system that the economists of that time believed would save the world.

Dad told me how the price of fuel climbed as demand increased and supply stealthily declined, then spiked in the summer of 2015 when gasoline topped eight dollars per gallon—if you could find a wet pump. He called the new economic order the "World Without Oil." Others just called it a continuation of the Twenty-Twelve Depression.

I remember that some people claimed 2015 was the year when the world went to hell—energy-wise, that is—not Sammy-wise. Canada cut back on the oil and gas they would ship to the U.S. Mexico needed all they could produce and only shipped oil to the U.S. in direct exchange for refined fuels. The depression kept the economy headed downhill.

In 2014 an outbreak of a new strain of flu began in the flood-ravaged slums in Bangladesh. This Neu-Flu spread across Asia and into Africa over the next two years. Dad told me how the U.S. kept the disease outside its borders until 2016, when a flood of refugees from Mexico carried the virus into California. By that time doctors in the U.S. had produced a vaccine; else things could have been worse.

Dad's position in the state government got us family priority vaccinations, so we stayed healthy, but Mom told me how many of our neighbors had no choice but to fight through the sickness without vaccinations. I heard Mom tell her mother on the phone, "My best friend, Margie, just died of the flu, and Tom says more than two billion people around the world have died; three million here in California alone and another twenty million down in Mexico. It's awful." Afterward, she laid her head on her arms and cried for a long time.

Living in downtown Sacramento at that time protected us from the floods. The El Nino weather pattern peaked again in early 2018, then remained active and generated the storms that pounded California for days on end, causing the winter floods of 2019.

Flood water destroyed most of the houses and businesses north of the American River on the other side of town. That land, except for the South Natomas development, had remained as open fields through the turn of the century because of concerns that the river levees would fail in a major flood. Dad said the city fathers rezoned the area in 2003 when they gave in to the growing political pressure from developers. During the housing boom of the next four years, a hundred thousand people moved into the developments, built on what had once been flood channels and rice paddies. When the floodwaters of the Sacramento River reclaimed the land fifteen years later, those people became homeless.

Afterward, city fathers talked about raising the levees and rebuilding the area, but apart from a few shanty settlements, the state and federal government used the lack of available insurance as the lever to force people to move to higher ground up around Folsom and down toward Stockton. After another twenty years, when the storms grew worse and sea levels rose, Folsom and Stockton flooded.

Grandpa and Grandma Hardy lived in Martinez, down next to where the Sacramento River flowed into the San Francisco Bay. They visited us one afternoon for my fifth birthday, and Grandpa Hardy told me and my folks all about the 2019 floods. "The heavy winter storms started in November and continued through February," he said. "Contra Costa County recruited a bunch of us county workers to go up into the Sacramento Delta to fight the floods, mostly to shore up the levees protecting the islands that carried the county's aqueduct. Back in those days our county's main water supply came from the Sierra Nevada Mountains and ran right near the Sacramento River."

He showed us some great flood photos on Dad's computer. "The storm poured rain on us for over seven weeks. More than once we received five plus inches of rain in a single day. The weather guys said a series of five-thousand-year storms hit northern California, like it had never happened that bad before. Most of us knew that global weather change had created a bigger El Nino and Pineapple Express, which were bringing far more warm air across the Pacific than in the past."

Grandpa explained his job. "We worked levee repair on a number of the islands, trying to plug all the leaks, but our efforts didn't do much good. We fought more and more levee sags and water boils as the waters rose and more rain saturated the ground."

"Then in mid-February, the Concord Fault ripped through the county with a 6.9 magnitude earthquake." He raised his hands into the air and shook them as he exclaimed, "Every levee in the delta failed in an instant. The ground shook from San Francisco to Auburn and from Fresno to Red Bluff. Five of our crews—with fourteen workers each—disappeared when the mud levees melted right out from under them as the ground shook. I listened to them screaming on the radios, but we couldn't do anything to help."

He shook his head and his eyes clouded. "We rescued three men, but the others disappeared without a trace. They never had a chance." I still remember how Grandpa stopped and swallowed.

Mom brought some cookies and coffee in from the kitchen to break the strain. They helped.

Grandpa went on to tell us how seven of the delta islands merged into one huge inland lake and marsh, forming the first Sacramento Sea. Within a month the whole area filled with brackish backwater from the San Francisco Bay. "The tidal currents running back and forth through the Carquinez Straits, separating the San Francisco Bay from the new Sacramento Sea, flowed close to twenty knots at times."

Dad added, "Yeah, that sea made a mess of things for the whole state of California. After the earthquake, the California Aqueduct that had carried fresh water down to Los Angeles couldn't get anything from the Sacramento River but brackish water."

Dad continued, "Southern California had already cut back on water usage when the Colorado River flows dropped by 60 percent two years earlier. Now the water from the north state tasted bad, and folks in the southland learned to live with salt water or do without. The people around LA suddenly understood the fragility of their water supply. One report I read said that migrations north and east out of the Los Angeles basin at that time jumped to as high as ten thousand a day."

Grandpa broke a cookie in two and handed me half. "I'm surprised anyone stayed down there."

Grandma Hardy picked me up. "Hey, the earthquake was sort of fun." She bounced me on her knee and smiled. "That's how it felt in the earthquake." She tickled my ribs then hugged me.

"Your grandfather left me home all alone when he went to work on the levees. Then early one morning there was a moan that started underneath the house." She moaned and then made a roar. "The ground shook. Pictures fell off the walls, and the TV fell onto the family room floor. The shaking lasted more than a minute, but it seemed like forever. Our house stood up pretty well, and I wasn't hurt. I turned off the gas and cleaned things up and then helped our neighbors fight their fires and repair their fences.

"I stayed in the house after the big quake and during all the aftershocks that followed. Mike made it back after about four weeks. He still had his job with the county, and they convinced us to stay in Martinez."

Grandpa said, "Many people in the East Bay just pulled up stakes and left their homes to go inland to the FEMA camps. Trouble is they didn't find much of anything there, except a place to sleep on the ground and a meager supply of fresh water and local food. The only jobs they found were with the work gangs."

He told us of the problems for those who stayed in Martinez. "We who remained got food from the county, but we had to get along with brackish water because all the aqueducts had been destroyed. Luckily, your grandmother and I had a reverse osmosis water system so whenever there was enough electrical power we could make drinking water. We still do that."

A few months later, I read on the Internet about San Francisco and the other cities around the Bay during that time. They built desalination plants and recycled their waste-water into drinking water to make up for their losses. They tried to catch up, but they never had enough power. People left in droves, mostly moving up and down the coast and into the valleys. Only Oakland held its own, but it started to become self-sustaining more than ten years earlier, so it had a head start.

The ProfSir said, "Puter, please pause again.

"You will find old records in our museum telling about the early twenty-first century and how nature beset the region called the San Francisco Bay and Sacramento. Sam's record tells us that the formation of the Sacramento Sea was a sudden event when an earthquake destroyed a levee system that society had built in the Sacramento River delta. Our studies at the university indicated it took place over time as the sea level rose, so this is new information.

"We must all remember that nature does not always act slowly. Sometimes, it acts catastrophically and fast. Puter, continue."

To save on fuel in 2017, Mom and Dad purchased a hybrid auto that ran on E-85—fuel composed of 85 percent ethanol. Then biofuel production peaked in the USA. The expanding Midwest drought and the depletion of the Ogollala Aquifer along the base of the Rocky Mountains wiped out much of the corn and soybean harvest. As the ethanol supply dropped and the country had to buy more and more ethanol from Brazil, E-85 fuel prices climbed even faster than old-style regular gasoline. Like so many others, Dad traded for an all-electric vehicle with an ammonia/hydrogen fuel-cell boost in 2020.

The boom in natural gas drilling lasted for a while, but in the end the energy required to drill those wells began to exceed the amount of energy that could be extracted, and the great natural gas bubble burst. At least the gas wells continued to produce feedstock for the plastics and fertilizer industries, though many clamored for the gas to be used for automotive fuel.

As fuel supplies dropped, demand continued to rise, and the price of transport fuel skyrocketed even higher. Four things happened: In 2020 the price of gasoline climbed above ten dollars per gallon. The government imposed strict fuel rationing to ensure critical commodities could be delivered to emergency services around the country. The number of vehicles driving on the roads dropped by over 80 percent. And the railroads staged an even bigger comeback as the least expensive alternative for shipping long distances over land.

People still traveled, but they did it much less and only for good reason. Nobody flew anymore except for the military or for really critical business.

Mom's parents, Grandpa and Grandma Boone, lived north of Yuba City near Gridley between the Sacramento and Feather Rivers. The Concord earthquake did not affect them very much. They had a farm and raised cherries and peaches. I remember when I was six, right after Dad bought his new E-car, he decided we should go live with my grandparents during the summer and help with the fruit harvest. He made telecommuting arrangements with the state so he could work on his job from most anywhere.

To establish a business reason for the travel, Dad contracted with a Chinese jobber to deliver a load of product to a hardware store in Gridley. He loaded up the new electric car and a small trailer with boxes and sacks of goods. We left early one April morning and drove north on old Highway 70.

I still remember how the roads shook our car pretty awful—nowhere near as bad as they later became over the years—but they were still full of potholes and broken concrete sections. Dad explained to Mom and me, "At my department's recommendation, California stopped maintaining secondary roads three years ago because raw materials like asphalt and concrete cost too much. They require too much energy and create too much CO_2 to manufacture. Last year California decided that with so much less traffic on the roads, they could eliminate road repair projects on all roads and do away with new road construction."

Dad took four hours to drive that hundred-mile trip. Mom and I suffered miserably for his department's decision.

I had a great time working on the farm that summer, and I learned a lot of useful things, but Mom and Dad always seemed worried. I heard Dad telling Mom and her folks, "My department is hearing reports that the federal government is finally admitting that the climate models used in the past have been far short in their estimates for ice melting on Greenland and in the Antarctic. The rise in sea level is going to be far worse than expected. In addition, the ocean currents seem to be going out of control. Things are happening that they did not expect."

Later I searched the Internet about the stoppage of the ocean's water conveyor system and found an old report from the Department of Defense. It said the Gulf Stream in the Atlantic might no longer take warm water up to Greenland and around to England anymore, and temperatures in the

British Isles and northern Europe could plummet. In a world of global warming, England could freeze like Siberia. They said that paleoclimatic evidence suggested that the altered climate patterns could last for as much as a century, as they did when the ocean conveyor collapsed 8,200 years ago, or, at the extreme, as long as 1,000 years like they did during the Younger Dryas period, which began about 12,700 years ago when the glacial melt suddenly dumped fresh water into the Atlantic Ocean down the St. Lawrence River.

Dad explained to us, "The forecasts are that this effect on the Pacific currents means we will be seeing even worse drought conditions develop here in California and across all the western states. In the midst of this drought, we'll also be getting horrendous winds and huge rainstorms."

I remember when Grandpa Boone asked, "But how could the government have been so far off? Didn't they know what was happening with the ocean currents?"

Dad explained, "No one in the government will take a strong position because the climate change skeptics keep arguing against all the research. And they have big backers and bigger pockets.

"But the scientific community pretty well understands what is going on. Overall, the earth is still collecting heat, and the average worldwide temperature is continuing to climb. The heat is collected mostly in the waters along the equator. Ocean currents help distribute that heat to the north and south poles. If the earth has to rely solely on the atmosphere to carry the heat north and south, the air is a lot less efficient. That means during the winter, the cold of the Arctic night can come down into the mid-northern latitudes without the moderating influence of the ocean currents. It also means that with the bigger temperature differentials, the winds will be blowing harder."

With my brain's capacity for total recall, I can remember every exact word spoken, but as a kid of six I did not understand all of the discussion at the time. Now I know much more of what happened, and Dad's comments were right on. The storms that later came down from the north sure proved him right.

That fall Mom enrolled me in public school. She wanted more time alone to do her tutoring work. Up to then I was a stay-at-home kid and had not been exposed to many of my peers, other than a few neighborhood friends I ran around with. I remember the start of school as a very traumatic time. I peed in my pants because I didn't know how to tell the teacher I needed to go to the bathroom.

Then, as the other kids began to study reading, I scanned the books the teacher supplied and asked for something worth reading. Several teachers tested me and found I could read at the seventh-grade level—the result of my surfing Wikipedia so early in my life—so they sat me in front of a computer and let me surf wherever I wanted to go, at least after I figured out the way around their parental controls.

About that time my mental powers expanded even more. I could easily integrate current information with what I knew from before. I began to study logic and learn more about scientific methods that produced rational answers rather than depending upon optimism, authority, and magic to explain things. Whenever a teacher tried to tell me something, I always had a response, and most often it was not the answer the teacher wanted to hear.

The teachers didn't know what to do with me, and I didn't know what to do with the teachers. After a time we just tolerated each other. That uneasy standoff lasted until Mom took me out of public school.

Sacramento had once been called "The City of Trees," but the growing shortages of fuel and power changed that forever. The city fathers told us to conserve and stop watering our shrubs, trees, and lawns—and the greenery began to die. The city remained a nice place, and I had lots of fun as a kid roaming around the old capital buildings and museums and down along the riverfront, but I remember how it all became very dry and dusty when it wasn't pouring rain.

The city began as a mining supply town but turned into a railroad one, though train traffic fell after the start of the Twenty-Twelve Depression. Then, as the fuel prices climbed even higher and long-haul trucking became too expensive, the railroads staged a comeback. My new buddies from public school and I had a great time walking the rails and trouping through the train yards looking for youthful treasures, like an old railroad spike. Once in a while we even hitched a ride in a freight car down to Stockton and back. Mom would have killed me if she had known.

Some fools expressed jubilation in 2019 with the news that Iran had become a net importer of fuel. The U.S. and Iran had been at each other's throats for decades, and the PSA people (that's the Party of Social Authority) celebrated that Iran was getting its "comeuppance," as some put it. Most people failed to realize that this meant the supply of available oil exports had once again dropped, to the detriment of all those countries wanting to import oil, like the U.S.. We had already lost our Mexican oil supply, and with the exports from Saudi Arabia dropping like a rock, we were down to the oil and gas we could beg from Canada and Nigeria to supplement our homegrown resources.

The first seven years of my life centered on my Mom and Dad, who sheltered me from the outside world, except for my buddies in the rail yards. My perspective changed after I turned eight.

Dad took me on a railroad train ride up to Sutherlin, Oregon, to visit with his grandparents: my Great-Grandpa Sam Hardy and Great-Grandma Alice. The train traveled through the Sacramento Valley and into the Coastal Range, and I saw the mountains between the valley and the Oregon coast. So many peaks were covered with parched, dry, and blackened trees. We could see a few green trees on some of the higher peaks, but most looked yellow or brown, like they had died. Dad explained, "The pine beetle infestation has pretty well wiped out the forests." In the distance we could see huge plumes of smoke from the big forest fires raging along the California-Oregon border, cleansing the beetle infestation.

When I saw my great-grandparents for the first time, I thought they looked almost dead—so old and frail. Medical science and good genes had allowed them to live too long. Now that I am approaching their age, I understand so much better how they must have felt.

Great-Grandpa Hardy tapped his chest and proclaimed, "Sammy, I'm eighty-six years old. Lots of people think I'm just a piece of copralite, you know, the fossilized remains of a dinosaur turd, but I am really just an old fart with a long memory." He laughed and coughed.

From the start Grandpa wanted to laugh and talk about how the weather had changed. He chuckled as he described how he and Grandma Alice once lived in a beautiful resort in the high desert of southern California and told me, "I warned the people that lived in our RV park that the weather would turn hot and dry, and the land around us would return to desert. I told them that if our park ever lost electricity, we could not pump water out of our wells, and our paradise would turn to hell. Some listened, but most said they couldn't do anything about that, so why bother."

He laughed like an old pirate as he related, "It was Thanksgiving in the year before you were born when we lost electricity from the Elsinore Quake, and some of my neighbors started to worry. When the water in the storage tanks ran out, all of them started to panic. After two weeks, when the vegetation around the park began to die, they all started to talk about moving out, but too many had set their roots deep. They couldn't move their rigs, and they watched their heaven turn to hell around them, just like I had said it would.

"But your great-grandmother and me—we had prepared and made plans." He bent toward me, looking like a conspirator. He whispered, "We made arrangements to move here in Oregon, to be in a place with running water that would continue to have water in the future.

"A couple of months after the quake, we loaded everything we cared about into our trailer, hooked it up to our old truck, and headed up Interstate 5 to this park in Sutherlin. The trip was damned expensive, what with the seven dollars per gallon they were charging for diesel fuel by that time, but we made it. Made it before the fuel prices really went out of sight. We were seventy-eight years old. I think that was pretty good for a pair of old farts—don't you agree?" He leaned back and laughed again, then coughed from the dust blowing through his trailer atop a hard gust of wind.

That trip to see my great-grandparents introduced me to Sutherlin, where I now live seventy-six years later in the year 2099. It was a nice RV park back in 2023; now it is a run-down cemetery of old trailer remains. Today, the only things you can see are flattened, vine-covered mounds that are now homes for a bunch of rats. Still, those remains hold many useful pieces of salvage. It is a good place.

Grandpa Hardy persisted in telling me how back at the beginning of the twenty-first century some people like him tried to warn the world of the coming bad times with resource depletion and climate change and a corrupt financial system, but no one would listen. "They called us Doomers," he said. "Some scientists talked about peak oil, where the demand for liquid energy would outstrip the supply and the price of fuel would skyrocket, but big corporations and the government said such an idea was hogwash—it was all a big scare. Then we began to see fuel prices rise, and people finally realized there could be a problem, but a problem most thought they could overcome. They figured King Technology would save their collective asses." I remember Dad's face turned red when Grandpa made that statement. Dad still believed technology would find a way.

Grandpa continued, "They forgot three things. The first was that our financial system had been created as a house of cards built on debt, and it would not stand. Second, inventions couldn't be turned into products as fast as society needed them. And last was that with the rising price of energy, the U.S. kept turning its currency into worthless pieces of paper. Those countries with anything valuable tried to live high on the hog just like us guys in the industrial world. They increased their consumption and ate up most of the added production they said they could squeeze out of their oil and gas fields.

"The net result was that the amount of hydrocarbons that could be exported by the largest oil producers to the rest of the world peaked around 2005 then started falling at about 2 percent per year." Grandpa sort of stared into the distance, like he was reading a sign.

"By 2015 the worldwide export rate was dropping 3.5 percent every year. Mexico stopped shipping oil to the USA about 2014—they used everything they could pump inside their own country, and now it is decreasing at over 5 percent per year.

"Sammy, do you know that two years ago in 2021 the available exports of oil from other countries amounted to less than half of what this country needed—or maybe I should say wanted. Any country with some kind of internal energy reserves made up the difference with coal and gas and nuclear and the like, and that only made things worse with climate change." He laughed again. "Those countries that didn't have the reserves are now bankrupt and having famines. They've no choice but to let their people starve."

"Why don't they just pump more oil?" I asked. "Then everyone could have what they need." How naive I was as a young boy. Of course, my talent for rational thought was just beginning to come into play.

Grandpa Hardy frowned at me, shook his head, and yelled, "Boy, don't you understand?" I began to shrink back under his stare. "Everyone had already pumped out the easy oil, and it takes a lot more energy to pump what's left, provided they even know how to do it. And there just isn't that much left. The oil producers have no way of keeping up with the demand." He laughed again, like he thought the problems facing the world were funny. I realized he laughed at most everything that was bad.

"Without as much oil available, those countries in the world that import oil have no choice but to outbid each other to secure their supplies. They might have devised other sources of energy, but they should have started at least ten years earlier to be ahead of the game. Some, like our country, procrastinated for so long that we're in a real mess. We import too much oil; we can't wean ourselves of the habit. We are addicts."

I said, somewhat proudly, "But I saw on the TV that we're solving our energy problem with biofuels and natural gas and nuclear plants. Peak oil is not a problem."

He frowned and stared at me for a moment. "You're a little bit right, Sammy. We have made some progress, but our real problem is we have hit a peak in imports, not a peak in oil. And resource limitations are only the tip of the iceberg. As early as 2006, 95 percent of the scientific community accepted the fact that man-created CO_2 and other greenhouse gases were causing global warming, and the resulting impacts on the world's environment would be catastrophic. But again big business and politicians fought those concepts tooth and toenail. We had water, food, and population problems coming along on top of everything else. The human race had become the scourge of the planet."

I remember how all that was pretty heavy for an eight-year-old, and I started to cry.

He ignored my crying and again yelled at me, "Even now, here in 2023, there are many folks in this country of ours who say we have the right to keep all the perks of living that we have known in the past. But young man, there is simply not enough energy available to allow that. There is not enough water or food for everyone, even in this country, to lead the life everyone is leading. There are too many people, especially those who say we must "stay the course," who are still in a state of denial."

I cried, "I won't stay the course, Grandpa. I promise I won't." He patted me on the back and gave me a hug. "I know you won't, Sammy. You won't have the chance." He turned and stomped back into the kitchen. I lay down on the couch and buried my head in a pillow.

The next evening, in our last serious conversation, Grandpa Hardy told me in a calmer voice, "Sammy, a thousand years from now, what we do today will make little difference. The U.S. citizens and government could have made a big difference back when this problem started, but we didn't. We could have made a significant difference in 2008 by choosing a government truly devoted to solving the problem, but we didn't. We could even make some small difference today if we would stop the bickering and attack the problems directly, but we aren't even doing that. In a few decades, the civilization that I have known, along with its people, will be gone, but the Earth will go on—it will just be a lot hotter and less friendly than it is now."

"What about me, Grandpa?"

"Sammy, I have great hopes for you. You have good blood in you. You have a share of my genes. Your mom says you're a genius, and your dad is teaching you a lot of survival and sustenance skills, even though you may not know them for that. Learn what you can, especially about the basics. Learn how to live off the land and how to plant seeds and make things grow. Learn how to make and use simple tools. Do the best you can, and if you are resilient and adaptive enough, there is a chance you will survive. If you are bright enough, you might make it through the bottleneck and be one of the few that survives the next seventy-five years."

The next morning Great-Grandpa and Grandma Hardy drove us down to the railroad station on the coast in Reedsport, and Dad and I left on the train, heading south to return home to Sacramento. They waved as we left the train station, and it was the last time I saw either of them.

I still recall most of the words that Grandpa Hardy spoke, and I now understand from personal experience what he was talking about. I have paraphrased a few of his words with what I now understand to be true. He told me in 2023 that our society knew of the problems as they started. They could have done so much, but they didn't. They would not relinquish their beliefs and myths that everything would work out for the best. They would not recognize reality, and instead they chose to live their life as if nothing could stop it. They left my generation with only one choice: sleep in the bed our forefathers had made for us.

What I heard from Great-Grandpa Hardy made a huge impression on me, and it spurred my rational mind into high-gear. I began to recognize that the habits of accepting myths and beliefs without question could not work in this new world. But I did not understand how much it mattered until a long time later. By then it was too late.

//////// \\\\\\\\

Sam's voice stopped. "End of file Chap-2," the Puter said.

"So class, what more have we learned about Sam Hardy? Has he told us more than we knew about the world during the Great Collapse of civilization? Is he part of our ancestry? SueJan, what do you say?"

The young girl shifted and shrugged, "I believe he must be part of the family from which we Neu-humans came. His story of his life as a child is in so much more detail than anything I have ever heard. It tells us so much about what we must do to be sure this does not happen again. The world can never support such a population that lives as extravagantly as it did."

CarlJu raised his hand, and when recognized said, "The people of the twenty-first century never learned to conserve their resources and use renewable supplies. They wanted to have everything without thinking of the future."

DanJo added, "I read how the minds of the human race at that time could not distinguish reality from what they wanted to be real. Most spent their lives in denial of the problems that faced them."

CosandJo held his hand above his head and waited for ProfSir Elder-Jan to recognize him. Finally, he said, "Somehow, I still think Sam Hardy must be The Old Man told about in the *Book of J*."

The ProfSir scowled, "CosandJo, you are one who is now trying to make reality be what you want rather than what it is. You are acting more and more like a throwback to those who came before us."

Chapter 3: Adolescence

June 8, 2024

The ProfSir looked over his group of young archaeologists gathered in the big tent after the evening meal.

"You all worked very hard today on the dig along the Umpqua River. We know Sam must have spent some of his time in this area with his tribe from Sutherlin, but that is still in the future. This evening you will hear Sam tell of his adolescent years. His life experiences differ from yours in so many ways, but I think you will identify with many of his emotions.

"Puter, please say to us the next file, Chap-3," said ElderJan.

There was the time in June 2024 that Mom stamped her foot on the kitchen tiles and screamed, "I am not sure if I should beat you to within an inch of your life, or kick you out the door forever. You've turned into a sleazy-minded, nasty, smart-alec bastard." I guess I upset Mom more than usual the time that neighbor lady reported how I sassed her when she found me practicing doctor with her seven-year-old daughter. That episode taught me that pre-teens should not play doctor, or at least not get caught.

Once I began to act like a teenager, Mom decided she should home-school me. She took my hand and led me to the school and told the principal, "Sammy is a child prodigy who has surfed the Internet from the age of two and read the entire Wikipedia before he turned four. I think it is best that I handle the rest of his education." She straightened her back to show her resolve, and the principal smiled and rubbed his eyes. I knew he was pleased that I would not be there anymore. He and I had our differences.

Mom didn't do much for my schooling. I did it for myself on the Internet. I even created some alias identities and started taking college level courses. I always found learning to be exciting and easy and spent lots of time on the computer reading everything I could find, some of it pretty graphic.

Meje held up her hand, and the ProfSir said, "Puter, please pause."

Meje asked, "Sammy talks like everyone had access to this Internet, and that is where all the knowledge came from. What was it? Did that really happen?"

"Meje, at the start of the twenty-first century civilization used a huge network of what they called telecommunications. That network supported a knowledge base called the World Wide Web that used a messaging protocol they called the Internet. It was one of the most amazing inventions of the time, and people in that era took it all for granted. We have some recordings of the knowledge that could be found on that network, but not everything that was there.

"Today we do not have an Internet because we do not know how to create such a telecommunications network. We have lost the technology required to build all the micro-electronics needed. When we are lucky, we find some of the knowledge from that time, such as this recording of Sam's memoirs. Finding knowledge that helps in our quest is one of the purposes of this expedition."

She asked, "Will we ever have something like the Internet again?"

"I don't know. Maybe we can learn enough about the previous civilization to recreate some of it, but it will take a long time." He shook his head, then said, "Puter, continue."

Sacramento, where we lived, experienced persistent shortages of foods in 2024. Stores offered more and more locally grown vegetables and grains, and the goodies that I liked disappeared, like chocolate. It cost too much to ship food in from other places like southern California or Mexico. Shipments of food from overseas became less available around the time I was born. Dad assured us we would not starve because we lived near good farmland, but the local food tasted so boring.

To Mom's dismay, I became an adolescent at the age of nine-and-a-half. I grew two inches during autumn, my voice cracked, and my sweat stunk. With a whole new cocktail of hormones coursing through my body, my time as an adolescent proved exciting and eventful. However, I don't remember it as being a very pleasant time.

There was another big change in my brain. All of a sudden, I became aware of the pitiful world around me and how much I didn't fit in. Everyone espoused their own preconceived idea of how things worked or should work, and simple logic showed how the vast majority were all wrong. Every time a new news item came along, they would change their minds on what caused the problems. Most people never seemed to be capable of rational thought.

But my new body changed even faster than my mind. After my tenth birthday, all my clothes shrank one size every month. I started popping buttons.

One day Mom took me shopping to buy clothes. She and I walked three miles to the Wally World. My arms and ankles stuck out like a scarecrow, and kids along the way laughed at me. I threw chunks of pavement at them until Mom grabbed my arm.

The store's clothes racks stood almost bare and nothing fit—thank goodness, because I could see how the prices exceeded Mom's budget. What few salespeople we saw in the store looked bleak and worried. One woman told us, "The mills in China shut down, and our shipments are not arriving as planned. The manager says it's temporary, but I'm looking for another job."

The store offered no real supply of clothes or anything else. China had dried up as our country's major source for cheap goods. Maybe the mega-drought they experienced had shut them down. Maybe it was the cost of shipping their product to our shores. Whatever the reason, we saw big-time effects in the U.S. retail space.

Walking back home empty-handed, Mom saw a hand-lettered sign on a light pole for a yard sale down a side street, and we went there. She picked over the clothes scattered around the porch, separated out several pieces, and asked the woman running the sale, "I see your younger son is about three sizes smaller than the clothes my Sammy is wearing. Would you trade what my boy has on, plus another four shirts and three pairs of shorts of the same size, for those three pair of jeans, these jockey shorts, a couple of wool shirts, and these two pairs of worn sneakers." The woman thought a moment then said yes if she got ten dollars to boot. Mom bargained some more and picked up a brand new hand-knitted sweater for herself.

Mom sent me to this woman's bathroom where I put on my new clothes and came out looking and feeling like a clown. I had grown from three sizes small to four sizes large. It took me a whole year to fill out those rags. The good and bad thing is that I wore them until I turned fourteen-and-a-half, and by then the clothes had turned to tatters.

I never told Mom about my gambling. She didn't believe in that kind of "sinning" as she called it, but I became one of the red-hot online gamers and won some big pots. I could only guess how much it would upset her to find out her ten-year-old son played as an avatar named Fearless Fogger and won a ten-thousand-dollar Texas hold 'em tournament in Bermuda. And from that beginning, my online persona became rich and famous.

By the age of eleven, I was an accomplished carbon trader. The government passed the first carbon rationing law in 2020, and every family and company got a carbon account and received magstrip cards to use for purchasing fuel, electrical power, and food-shipping surcharges. You started each month with an allotment of carbon units you could use, and as you did your purchases you swiped your card to debit your C-account for the amount of carbon used to produce what you purchased. It was all pretty simple unless you ran out of your allotment for the month. Then you could freeze or starve to death for all the system cared.

Dad used his own C-Card as part of his job, but I took care of Mom's C-Card for her. She never liked monitoring accounts on the Internet. I loved it.

Part of the government plan let you trade, buy, and sell carbon units with other people or companies, most often on the Internet. People valued the C-units like money, and when you traded them you could get goods or money credits in return.

I created another Internet identity—a ditsy twenty-two-year-old girl named Prudence—with her own website. I made up that she lived with the old lady across the street, the one I ran errands for, so I could watch her mailbox. Then I used part of my poker winnings to set Prudence up with a money account and shopping cart. Next I linked Mom's C-Card account to Prudence's commercial account. I handled all the paperwork and details. I am proud to say Mom never experienced a problem with her carbon card. She told everyone how perfect the system worked.

I shopped around and found people who didn't like the carbon rationing idea, so they sold their units cheap. I also set up a little online store where people could buy stuff I found in yard sales around the neighborhood or on the Internet. They could buy these with their carbon units or with money; I dealt in either currency. I also did a lot of bartering with the local people.

Shipping turned out to be the real problem. It cost an awful lot. The remains of the U.S. Postal Service continued to be the cheapest, but sometimes it took weeks to go even a hundred miles. And the rates kept climbing until that service almost stopped.

The business in carbon units picked up, and I watched for notices of people looking for C-Units, often because they wanted to travel or maintain some kind of fuel-guzzling HUV. Some people even wanted to buy an airplane ticket. Air travel cost almost a whole year's C-Unit allocation for a plane ticket across the country, so I collected a lot of cash for that kind of sale.

Once in a while I ran across something really nice for Mom and ordered it sent to our house as if she won a prize from a TV game show. She couldn't remember entering the game show contests, but she never sent her winnings back.

By 2026 most of the Greenland coastline lay bare during the summer months, and on the satellite images you could see the traces of the individual glaciers in the interior. Worse yet, the breakup of the glaciers supplying the western Antarctic ice sheet accelerated. The USGS announced that the sea level rose thirty centimeters since the beginning of the century, and that lifted the toes of the glaciers enough that they moved and melted even faster.

Some scientists said that within the next twenty years, the sea level would rise as much as another meter. They added that they were sorry their earlier estimates for a one meter rise in the next eighty years had been wrong. The thermal expansion of the oceans caused even more havoc and added to the uncertainty. It showed how useful "sorry" was.

The climate kept going from bad to worse. The annual rainfall totals in the temperate climates dropped to record low levels, and in 2025 the mega droughts that began in China and India sealed the fate of another billion souls, this time from starvation.

In the Midwestern U.S., farmers pumped so much water to irrigate their fields of corn and soy beans to make bio-fuels that the Ogallala aquifer, containing tens of thousands of years of water runoff from the Rocky Mountains, began to go dry. Western Kansas and Nebraska turned into a patchy desert with sand dunes. I remember one report that the dry line marched eastward from the Rockies fifty miles every year. Farming disappeared from much of the plains, and over time, more and more of the ethanol and bio-diesel plants closed. The production of food grains dropped even faster.

TV carried pictures showing Shanghai, Tokyo, Amsterdam, Venice, and New York being inundated by the rising sea levels. Authorities estimated 50 million people would be displaced in the United States, 120 million in Bangladesh, 150 million in India, and 250 million in China. The state and federal governments curtailed all new development in coastal zones and even suggested people and industry evacuate early.

The people who lived along the coasts screamed for levees and dikes, ignoring the experience of New Orleans, which depended upon levees twenty years before. For the most part, governments could not find the funds to build the levees and dikes.

In 2025 California declared bankruptcy, and the U.S. economy pretty much ground to a halt. In November of that year, the U.S., Canada, and Mexico took the first steps at forming the consortium that would become known as the North American Federation, under the control of the Party of Social Authority, an outgrowth of the Occupy and Tea Party movements of 2013.

The PSA was an authoritarian nationalist political ideology. It advocated the creation of a totalitarian single-party state that sought to mobilize the masses of the nation through indoctrination, physical discipline, and family policy. It sprang from a coalition of the fundamentalist and ultraconservative groups that controlled the country during that time. Both the socialists who wanted to support everyone and the marketeers who wanted total freedom of choice lost to those who simply wanted to control what was going on.

Reports from the White House said the U.S. joined the NAF union for economic and energy coordination, but everyone in the know believed it to be a matter of controlling immigration.

The primary countries of North America did not want any more immigrants arriving from places like South America, Africa, or the Middle East. They constructed a new fence across the southern border of North Mexico, and all border travel stopped there. They restricted shipments of fuels from the Mexican oil fields, the Canadian tar sands, and the U.S. oil shales to uses within the new NAF. They still needed to import oil from the Middle East and Africa, most of it from Saudi Arabia and Nigeria, to feed the energy requirements of the 460 million residents of the Federation. The pandemic fatalities and dramatic drop in birthrates in Mexico cut the count down from the 535 million it would have been.

The following year, Russia took control of the EU for what some guessed to be the same reason as the consolidation of North America. Some called New Europe a marriage of convenience for Europe because of the pending collapse of the EU. Without Russia's energy resources, Western Europe's fate would be to become a wasteland. Russia ruled the roost with an iron fist after that.

China began to experience a series of wild internal problems with its people. The citizenry first tasted the perks we in the U.S. got at the beginning of the century, and when the cost of energy went out of sight, the government cracked down and took most of those perks away. The people grumbled, and reports of a civil war filtered into the news. As the spring of 2026 approached, drought conditions in China and India worsened, and we kept hearing reports of widespread rioting from the hordes that spread out across both lands searching for food and water.

Some estimated that with the food wars and pig-flu, China and India each lost over half of their population in the next three years. In time the populations of both China and India fell below one billion each from the pandemics, and the mega drought across Asia. The countries of Afghanistan, Pakistan, and Bangladesh dropped back into fundamentalist barbarism.

An amazing number of people in our country in 2026 still denied that our society had a problem with energy or weather or the economy. The world kept changing around them, and they just didn't know how to handle it. It took little effort on my part to make a fortune on their stupidity. I started small with my gaming profits, and before long built that stash into millions. I moved most of the money to off-shore accounts just to be safe.

At the end of August in 2026, Hurricane Gracie struck New York City. She came toward land as a Category 5 hurricane with winds over 150 miles per hour, but she relented and hit Manhattan as a slow-moving Category 4 storm. Gracie made 2011's Irene look like a spring shower.

I remember how Mom, Dad, and I sat glued to the TV throughout the night watching the satellite and radar images as the hurricane's eye wound its way up the coast of New Jersey across Long Beach, then veered into the Lower Bay just south of New York City. Early in the morning, it punched north into the Upper Bay and continued up the west side of the Hudson River. I can still remember TV pictures of the Statue of Liberty inside the eye, standing so peaceful in the sunrise.

The storm surge into the East River measured thirty-five feet. Water poured from the river into the surrounding countryside. Long Island disappeared under water, and over half of New Jersey flooded. When the storm ended, they reported fifty-three thousand people dead or missing, and authorities estimated over two trillion dollars in damage. I heard that the storm left more than eight million homeless, and the damage reached north past Albany all the way into Maine.

The hurricane destroyed the island of Manhattan. They never found enough money to pump out the subways.

ProfSir said, "Puter, pause here. Class, we have other records at the university telling of this event, when a great storm swept into the population center of North America. It devastated their economy as well as their society."

SamJan asked, "Was this expected?"

"It was well known that an event like this could happen, but it appears no one of importance did anything serious to protect against such an event. This was typical of the culture of this time."

"Were the effects as bad as Sam implies?" SamJam asked.

"Oh yes, this event marked the end of the United States of that time as the economic leader of the world. It had a terrible impact throughout the country and the rest of the world." He looked around for further questions, but there were none. "Puter, please continue."

Losing the financial center of the country—and maybe of the world—broke the back of the U.S. financial system. China and Saudi Arabia stopped using dollars in their trades, and the world no long denominated oil in dollars. They required gold or grain or some other solid commodity to complete any transaction.

My early decisions made me one of the lucky financial successes; I had moved all my funds out of New York to Sydney and Toronto the year before. I put most of my cash into gold equivalents. With things so unstable, I started another gold fund in Johannesburg, managed it over the Internet, and learned basic commodities trading firsthand.

My international funds continued to do well by any measure, and I possessed a good supply of Chinese Yuan and gold stashed away in a Singapore bank built high above the bay. Rising sea levels would not catch me.

In 2027 we heard of a new worldwide pandemic; they called it the pig-flu. Over the next three years it killed another estimated one-and-a-half billion people, the majority in Africa and the Far East. The Indonesian area experienced the highest percentage of casualties. The pig-flu got a foothold in Europe and Russia and along the U.S. east coast, but strict quarantines kept it out of California long enough for the vaccine to be developed.

Pig-flu counted as the third of the big pandemics. After the first two, the government assured everyone that they were in total control of the situation, and it would never happen again. For the ones unfortunate enough to catch the disease, they just blew smoke. This new pandemic proved just how little you could trust the government's word.

A few cases of pig-flu happened in Sacramento, most of them fatal, but state employees and their families received vaccinations within twenty-four hours, and our family remained safe. However, Grandma and Grandpa Hardy who lived in Martinez died in the pandemic. We later found out that my great-grandparents also died from the pig-flu up in Oregon.

In 2027 Chile, Brazil, and Argentina merged into the South American Federation under a little-known Brazilian Colonel, Alfredo Lopez. Their combined armies turned north to occupy Venezuela and Bolivia and take over the oil, gas, and tar fields. After a few demonstrations in Caracas, the Colonel's troops eliminated the Chavez gang and did not let the demonstrations continue. Caesar had outlived his time, and he disappeared without a trace.

The Middle East continued as the world's hotbed of violence, with sporadic wars cropping up every so often in the different countries between the different ethnic tribes and religious sects. Those countries still with oil to export continued to sell to the highest bidder, just so long as the buyer could pay in something other than U.S. dollars.

Israel had few fuel reserves, but they became very adept at conservation and generating non-petroleum fuels. They had to; their neighbors imposed a fuel embargo on the country. Israel occupied Lebanon and portions of Syria and Iran, but their annexations did not include significant oil reserves. But by 2018, they had developed the offshore gas fields in the Mediterranean and become one of the richer countries in the Middle East. They continued to trade with the U.S. and hold their neighbors at bay.

When the Saudi Arabian royal family lost control of their country, the factions began to fight amongst themselves. China sent its navy to get involved. That brought in a couple of U.S. carrier groups, and things got complicated and dicey. Some feared nuclear attacks, but the contestants fought the naval battle with conventional weapons. Within three hours about half of each Navy sank to the bottom of the Hormuz Straits. After that, everyone backed off, but no one knew what would happen next.

The Saudi's solved their own problem and executed a third of the royal family. The country closed its borders to pilgrims to Medina and Mecca, creating a tremendous uproar of protest among the Islamist sects.

Those northern portions of Africa with oil fields allied themselves with various Middle East countries. The remainder of Africa, decimated with disease and drought, suffered massive starvation and fatalities. By 2028 the population of Africa fell 80 percent from its level at the turn of the century.

Early in the twenty-first century, Australia had adopted stringent measures to control water and fuel usage. Even though they lost as much as 70 percent of the country's productive land to drought, the country held its own, using the few fossil fuels from along its northern coast for chemical feedstock as it built huge solar farms in the outback. The crisis grew so great that they even began the construction of six new nuclear plants.

Even though the rest of the world seemed to be falling apart, everything went well for me until the fall of 2029 when Mom's parents moved in. Grandpa Boone's fruit trees up in Gridley died because he could not contract to get enough water for them. The Sacramento and Feather Rivers ran high during the floods, then dropped to almost nothing when the rains quit, and the electricity to run the pumps didn't stay on very long. My grandparents sold their farm for a pittance and came to Sacramento to live with my folks.

By that time, at the age of fourteen, I stood over six-foot-four and weighed 145 pounds. I wore rags for clothes, so I fit into the current style. I took up a lot of room. Mom and Dad had relocated to a two bedroom apartment a year before, and they told me to sleep on the living-room couch, which was all of six feet long.

But the bad part was that I didn't know that Grandpa Boone knew so much about using a computer. Somehow he found out about my carbon trading on the Internet. He spoke to Dad, and I got a lecture on "don't do something that might get us all in trouble." Dad explained how the police were putting together plans to crack down on what they called a black market in carbon units.

In retrospect it turned out well, because Dad got me out of the market at the right time. I had sent out warnings, but a couple of my Internet trading buddies didn't strike their tents in time, and the cops confiscated their gear and tossed them into jail.

With a fink in the house, I lowered my profile. I transferred most of my carbon and gold accounts to a charitable trust that just happened to give out scholarships to smart cookies like me. I kept Prudence going to help Mom, but made sure no incriminating evidence could be found on my computer.

A month after Grandpa and Grandma Boone moved in, my folks received an official-looking letter that said, "Even at the age of fourteen, Samuel Julian Hardy qualifies for a fully-paid four-year scholarship at the University of California in Davis for a major of his choice, plus an option to fully pay for five years of graduate school."

My folks told everyone of their pride in me, but wondered how this charitable trust found me. I explained to them, "I applied over the Internet, and now my education won't cost you a thing." I puffed my chest out with pride.

I never told them how I had made a substantial contribution from one of my offshore accounts to this charity to buy my ticket out of the house. At the time I would do anything to escape the place.

"End of file Chap-3," the Puter said.

As the Puter stopped, CosandJo relaxed and let out his breath. He thought, *"That sounds so much like my life. People around me cannot understand me."*

The ProfSir cleared his throat. "Class, even back in that early civilization, the people understood the need for a good education, and they worked hard to achieve that goal. It seems Sam found a more innovative path to achievement.

"Now, about our plans. Tomorrow we will move our camp north to the Sutherlin area where CosandJo found his treasure. There should be some good salvage sites we can sample, and we can search the area where CosandJo dug up Sam's discs more thoroughly."

As ElderJan rose, turned, and walked out of the tent, CosandJo lifted his clinched fist into the air and muttered under his breath a quiet, "Yes, back to the source of our roots."

Chapter 4: UC Davis

January 24, 2030

CosandJo led the other twelve neophyte archeologists, three individuals and five pairs mounted on their own three-wheeled pedal carts, down the hill on the crushed rock path. He raced ahead, dodging the shrub growths filling the cracks. The line of tri-carts followed as he turned off onto the dirt field leading to the site where he had found the green box three days before. ProfSir ElderJan followed a quarter mile behind on his battery-assisted four-wheeled cart pulling the camp supply wagon.

As the younger archeologists arrived at the site and parked their carts, CosandJo led them up the hill to the mound where he had dug. He pointed to the hole that had held the treasure.

"Wait, wait," called ElderJan as he brought his cart to a stop. "I must be the first to survey the dig site. I must see what lies about and determine where we must search." He hurried over to the group and pushed to the front.

"Where was the box?" he demanded of CosandJo.

The boy pointed to the hole in the dirt from which he had pulled the box. "There. It was just under the surface and my digging stick hit it when I poked at the mound."

ElderJan dropped to his knees and carefully investigated the material near the hole. He pushed more clods aside and pointed. "Look, here are some small bits of artifact remains. We must collect these and determine what they might be." He began to organize his expeditionary forces to do a careful dig of the area.

"PaulJa, you and SueJu will come with me to set up our big tent down by the stream.

"The rest of you lay out the dig area like I taught you in Hudson Bay. Center the search on the mound where CosandJo found the box. We will dig here for up to three days and I would like to thoroughly investigate this mound down at least two feet and check the surface of the surrounding mounds.

"We are looking for all articles of human construction, including shards of building materials and remains of tools. We may be able to identify the foundation of the structure that stood on this location and learn something about it last occupants.

"I would like all of you to work on this dig location as long as there is still light. Tomorrow I will send some of you to explore the surrounding areas and search for salvage.

He turned back to his cart and lead his helpers on the way down to the flat beside the small stream.

Later, after the class had eaten their evening meal, they gathered in the tent and sat on their rugs. ElderJan said, "Today we will hear how young Sam Hardy began his collegiate education at the California University of Davis. He was fourteen years old at the time, only a year older than when you young folks are expected to begin your higher education. Most of his peers did not continue their education or they entered the universities at the age of eighteen. But we must realize that over the centuries we have experienced marvelous genetic improvements in the human race."

CosandJo asked, "Do we start earlier because we are really more intelligent, or do you simply force us to take these courses when we are younger?"

The ProfSir scowled at his nephew. "I believe our race is a significant advance in humankind, and you apprentices should be fully capable of handling the learning experience. You and all the other apprentices are told from the beginning that should you fail, you will be dropped from the educational program and sent to the farm labor program. We only expect people to accomplish to their level of capability. We force no one." He turned to the machine next to him. "Puter, please say to us the next file, Chap-4."

In January 2030 I entered the University of California, Davis, as a fourteen-year-old freshman. I moved out of my home into a coed dormitory on campus. What an experience. I now could do all the lab work I had missed in my earlier sex education courses.

With years of experience under my Mother's tutelage, plus my excursions on the Internet, I challenged all the lower-level graduation requirements and scored top honors on the placement tests. I chose a triple major in atmospheric sciences, chemical engineering, and economics. That way I got a lot of basic physics and chemistry as background for the meteorology and engineering, plus a good review of all the outdated and obsolete economic theories of the past twenty-five years.

From the beginning I soaked up knowledge like a carnivorous sponge in the ocean. What I learned over the Internet as a kid took place as a singular experience with a screen on the other side. Now the learning experience became a group effort, with different ideas coming from my fellow students and professors.

I still tracked news of the world and continued to spend lots of time on the Internet. Once away from the prying eyes at home, I resumed my dabbling in online trading and gambling.

The North American Federation, formed in 2026, moved in the expected ways. The combined governments of the U.S., Canada, and Northern Mexico stopped most of the immigration from Europe, South America, and the Caribbean. They imposed high tariffs on whatever could be produced by local industry. Protectionism was a law of the land.

The government kept making the wrong decisions on how to solve the problem of shortages of liquid fuels required for transport. Government and business just couldn't get the concept of efficiency, conservation, and local commerce through their heads, I guess because it conflicted so much with their archaic goals of continued growth using infinite resources.

Saudi Arabia sold us Middle East oil when no other country would, and as the situation worsened in Riyadh, people kept saying that that source would dry up in a few months. Of course, the available Saudi supplies had plummeted earlier by 65 percent from 2014 when Ghawar peaked and went into decline.

The Athabasca Tar Sands never became the reliable energy source the developers hoped. The water needed to extract the hydrocarbons in sufficient quantities to make the project pay off did not exist. The meager funds allocated to develop some new innovative way of extracting the energy without using more than you got back resulted in nothing. U.S. government teams began serious work on producing *in situ* SynFuel in Colorado, but again they needed more research and innovative ideas.

Geothermal, solar farms, and wind farms became a significant portion of our electrical supply, but the government still resisted making big investments in those technologies, even though they produced the minimum pollution and lasted the longest of all the choices. No political constituency representing those sources could demand the subsidies and offer contributions and support like those that continued for coal, nuclear, natural gas, and biofuels.

The countries of the NAF completed 137 coal-fired power plants in the early twenty-first century, most of them in Wyoming, Colorado, and Illinois. However, it took the reality of transport costs climbing out of sight before they realized that building the high-voltage power lines to transmit the electricity was more effective than using trains to carry the coal to where folks needed the electricity. One good thing happened: the government required that all coal burning plants do carbon sequestering from the start, but then they eased some of the restrictions as power became scarcer.

Another seven nuclear plants became operational, with three more on the way, but that did not come near meeting our demand. Energy consumption would be cut for lack of supply, a choice the Greens had pushed for over half a century. The country worked out a whole new economy with the biggest loser being the transport business.

Government began to encourage development of the thorium reactors. That technology provided a small unit for installation in a variety of places, and those reactors did a great job burning the wastes from the older reactors, but the rate of building the units could not keep up with the growing demand.

By 2030 everyone traded with what they called "locallars," or localized dollars, the product of the dropping of the U.S. dollar as the worldwide currency by the rest of the world in 2027. But in my economics coursework at the university, we based our comparisons in terms of 2010 dollars. I found it easier to see what happened if you compared the price of new apples with old apples, even when you found everything rotten to the core.

The government capped the price of oil with price controls at an equivalent of $225 per barrel in 2010 terms, and electricity at fifty cents a kilowatt-hour.

This compared to historical prices at the beginning of the century when the energy prices reached $20 per barrel and ten cents per kilowatt-hour. With my Internet contacts, I found that prices for fuel on the black market stood at $575 per barrel for oil and $2.80 for a kilowatt-hour. Fuel could be found if you demonstrated willingness and the ability to pay for it.

After spending two quarters in the dormitory at UC Davis, I found the coed scene to be too demanding for my young psyche, and I returned to live at home.

Part of my problem in the dorm was my tail. I had learned on the Internet that during the development of the human fetus, everyone has a tail, and except in a few rare cases it is absorbed back into the coccyx as the fetus develops. I learned later in my life that my four inch long vestigial tail covered with red hair was associated with the mutation that also changed the structure of the Hardy family brain.

Other members of my genetic family exhibited the same characteristic, and I would guess that my Great-Grandpa Hardy and all his progeny had the same tail. But in the old days it was removed at birth. For some reason, mine was not.

Some of the girls in the dorm found out about my tail and began spreading rumors. They described it as funny to all their friends, and some called it cute and wanted more than I could deliver. Such are the problems of a close society.

Commuting from Sacramento to Davis meant that I must learn to put up with my grandparents. That required the patience to just ignore their presence. Of course, by using the computer system available at UCD, Grandpa Boone's prying eyes could not see how or where I spent my time. The remote computing link to the university worked well and covered my tracks.

I handled the high price of commuting by riding my bicycle between the two cities, a one-way trip of twenty-two miles. Two-thirds of my classes could be handled over the Internet, so, thank God, I did not ride my bike to school every day. Even though it no longer rained much during the winter, the winds across the Yolo Causeway could be horrendous at times, and I hunkered down peddling the bike on those days.

Mom fed me good, healthy food, and riding my bike most of the time produced the muscle bulk for a big, strong kid. I stopped growing when I turned sixteen, after reaching six-five and a weight of two-twenty. I felt shy, though my large body, freckles, and the shock of curly red hair made everyone think of me as strong and outgoing.

As a university student, I became so involved in the learning process that I almost gave up the Internet trading game, but not quite. Using the facilities at the university, I still made six figure profits overseas every year without too much thought. I dabbled in simple trading strategies and took every course I could get into, trying to expand my education in a mental feeding frenzy.

As I began to take upper division courses at the university, I enrolled in several interesting classes that gave me the opportunity to discuss the deeper aspects of what I studied with the professors and other students. A whole new dimension opened up to me. My economics courses gave me a more accurate insight into what happened in our markets, and I learned how wrong-minded the economic theories driving the world from 2007 to 2015 had been. The economists of that time did not understand how economics worked. All their theories depended upon infinite resources and continued growth.

But the hedge fund managers and financial magnates understood how to game the system and shape policy so that they collected ever more of the wealth of the nation. Of course, they set things up so I could make my fortunes by following their leads, but the growing social unrest was a concern.

My teenage optimism took a hit when I found out that by 2011 the United States could not pay its bills. In fact, the whole world floated on a sea of debt. In all of my trading of financial instruments, I just moved hallucinatory wealth around. I realized my multi-million dollar accounts existed as vapor. My luck continued to hold only because many in the world still attached value to that vapor.

With my growing education also came the realization of the extent of the damage the human race did to our planet. But I could not come up with any good way to get out of the situation. One thing was for sure: things would get worse as we approached a time of survival of the fittest. The fittest would be those with the skills to live in the new world. I remembered my great grandfather telling me I might be smart enough to make it through the bottleneck, and I began to appreciate what bottleneck he had talked about. We were not there yet, but even then I knew it would happen soon.

I turned seventeen in 2032, during my senior year. My beard began to grow, along with all the other hair on my body. The hair on my face came in redder and curlier than my head. Few of the guys in my class shaved, and I, like many others my age, decided, what with the cost of heating water, that I could find a better use for my carbon units. I began trimming my beard every other week. I still do that today, though now it looks like my white face suffers from a bad case of the mange.

I completed my bachelor's degree in two-and-a-half years and entered graduate school that June at UC Davis, still on my fake scholarship. My nose remained on the grindstone. I allotted no time for waiting around or socializing. I absorbed information without giving any thought to what use it might be. I chose a graduate major in chemical engineering with a hydrocarbon specialty. That school received high marks at the university. I settled into the puritan life of a serious graduate student.

About this time I came to believe I could find some kind of solution that would save the world. My work on energy provided some real food for thought, and I became obsessed with finding a new energy source. In retrospect, I admit I had no chance for success; I was running on hope.

I continued to ride my bike to Davis from my folk's home every other day, because I worked in the Chem-E lab as a research assistant on several important experiments. Every other night I worked late and spent the night with friends in the department, or sometimes I slept on a cot in the lab.

My life changed in 2033 after I turned eighteen—I met Abby, a fifteen-old, just over two years younger than I. She had progressed through the educational system even faster than I and had reached her third year at the university, majoring in languages. She could speak six tongues, and everyone expressed admiration at how well she could curse in each of them.

It all began on one of those long nights working in the lab. Joe Bradley, a fellow grad student, and I took a break and headed out for a beer on the other side of campus. Joe happened to see three young girls walking across campus. "Hey," he whispered to me. "You're a big man on campus—in more ways than one." He often laughed and kidded me about my six-five frame. "Why don't you get us a date?"

I told him, "Joe, those girls are jail-bait—still in high school." But Joe said he recognized at least one of them from one of his senior classes. "Joe, quit kidding around," I said. "You're trying to get me in trouble." But as I looked over the petite girl in the middle with the long brown hair and bouncy step, I began to reconsider. Something about her turned me on.

Joe whispered in my ear. "You can do it. Go ask." He pushed me toward the girls. They stopped and stared at us. "Tell them you're from France and need directions."

So I sauntered up and did my best imitation of a French accent to say what I thought translated as, "Hi there, could you ladies give my friend and me some directions?"

The girl in the middle, the one who caught my fancy, began to laugh like mad and point her finger at me. "That is the worst imitation of French I ever heard," she cried. She sat down on the grass, kicked her heels, and giggled. "What are you? Some kind of hick from Fresno, or what?" she asked and giggled again.

I blushed and sat down on the slope beside her. "You know, you're right. I was born in Fresno, but now I live in Sacramento. Joe told me I could get your attention this way," I said, using my most proper California English.

She sat up and smiled looking me straight in the eye. "Well, it worked, and yes, I can give you directions if you need them, but just your company would be a lot more fun. Hi, I'm Abby." She reached out, and we shook hands. I still remember the tingle I got when our hands touched.

The five of us went on over to the pub for a beer. Joe made a point of becoming preoccupied with the other two girls, and paid Abby and me no mind. We chatted a bit and learned about each other, and then she asked, "Why don't you walk me home? I think my friends know how to keep your friend Joe busy tonight."

We enjoyed a beautiful walk in the May moonlight back across campus, and I held her hand. It turned out that she led me to her parent's house. I showed my reluctance, but she pulled me into the house and sat me down in the living room with her dad, who just happened to be Dean of the Agriculture Department. She joined her mom to work in the kitchen. Over the drone of her dad's voice lecturing me on the future of genetic grains for biofuels, I heard her talking with her mother. Snatches of their conversation came through the door, and one emphatic statement I heard her make sounded like, "… and I know he's the one I want. I found him, Mom. I found the guy I want."

I could not believe the revelation I heard, and I remember feeling befuddled and stupid the rest of the evening. Her dad said something about my working too long and needing rest, then he and her mom went to bed. Abby and I sat on the couch talking about our likes and dislikes and found to our amazement a large number of similarities. I began to worry about overstaying my welcome.

"I better go," I said and stood up.

Abby grabbed my hand and pulled me back down to the couch. "No, silly boy, you don't need to go. I want you to stay here with me. To make a long story short, I spent the whole night with Abby.

I quit bicycle commuting from Sacramento the next week, after Abby's sixteenth birthday party, and moved into her parent's home. My mom seemed concerned about the suddenness of my decision, but Dad told her to tend to her knitting. Abby's parents didn't seem to mind. Steven, her dad, said, "That's how couples get together these days; they're quick." Things changed so fast in our lives that extra time did not exist to make a choice— we went with what happened.

Nine months later I turned nineteen, and to celebrate the occasion, Abby and I moved out of her parent's place into our own studio apartment. We said some words in front of our friends like we were getting married, but we didn't bother with an official license or anything.

We lived together, but the messy state of the world prevented us from considering being a real family and having kids or anything like that. Our friends told us we picked the wrong time to get together, but I don't know think either of us could have remained sane and survived if we had not had each other to depend upon for support.

At that time in 2034, a lot of people still lived in a state of denial regarding climate changes. They believed technology would solve the problem, telling everyone, "Just be patient." People continued to ignore conservation and efficiency. "What I do doesn't make that much difference." All the warning signs flew in everyone's face, but no one listened. Too many kept arguing over how to find a replacement for the auto fuel now becoming so scarce, unwilling to give up anything.

In the fall of that year a huge forest fire destroyed the forests around Lake Tahoe. I heard one fellow say, "Most of the trees are already dead anyway, so what does it matter." However, the smoke backed into the Sacramento Valley, and I found it hard to breathe for the next three weeks.

The Arctic ice fields became history, and Greenland lost over half of its ice blanket. Antarctica continued to melt down, and the rise in sea level approached a full meter around the world. Storms ravaged the land and farming began to fail throughout the country. It had already failed big-time in the plains of the Mid-west, and now the problems extended into the south. The warming trend continued around the globe, but people became jubilant when rumors started that some research showed the increase in greenhouse gases leveling off. Unfortunately, they didn't understand that it was already too late.

Communications remained excellent throughout the world in 2034. Every-one in the U.S. watched television available by cable or satellite, or they used the total, ubiquitous Internet access available everywhere. Everyone could get instant access to information about every event that happened around the planet. If the newsrooms didn't cover it, some blogger would. That level of communication continued until the political situation changed in 2035.

In the first week of 2035, another round of mass riots struck in China, India, and Bangladesh. Early reports indicated that lack of food and water started the conflicts, and the riots grew and grew. China called out its army to put down riots in Singapore, and the fighting spread throughout the whole country. Soon the reporters and bloggers said every person must fight for himself. Apparently, according to some news analysis, another half of the population of China died in the two weeks of rioting that ensued. India experienced much the same.

In Bangladesh and Pakistan, the riots started after the monsoonal floods and the rumors of food and water hoarding in different neighborhoods. Surrounding neighborhoods invaded those suspected of hoarding, killing everyone there as they searched for the treasure. Those two countries lost 80 percent of their people. The killing only stopped when the few survivors grew too tired to continue.

ProfSir said, "Puter, please pause. Class, Sam is telling us first hand of the period when the die-off in the population of the earth approached its maximum rate. The riots and destructive weather added to the downward pressure from the pandemics on the population, and the 2030s marked the real end of the old human race. That was when the excesses of the past one hundred and fifty years caught up with the dominant race on the planet."

PaulaJa asked, "Was there anything that could have been done to save the human race at that time?"

"No, I don't think so. Some of you have already studied the history of this period at the university, and you understand how the forces were too strong. The ways of the world were too set. There was not enough food, there was not enough energy to produce food, there were not enough resources for a large number of humans to survive. We know from the archives at the university that the whole world had a very difficult time adjusting to the changing conditions."

The students looked uncomfortable. Hearing of the extinction that took place at that ancient time from someone who was there made it so much more immediate than hearing a dry lecture in a class.

The ProfSir said, "Puter, please continue."

Toward the end of the year, few news reports were coming from the rest of the world. My friends and I believed the NAF was censoring the news being reported.

We did hear of the outbreak of dengue fever in Taiwan and Japan. A group of doctors at the World Health Organization said the rising temperatures on those islands allowed the mosquitoes to spread north, carrying the dengue virus into new populations. With little genetic resistance to stop the spread of the disease, the infections decimated the populations of several Far East island countries.

Little news came from Europe, though the bloggers reported the EU to be near collapse. They told how cold weather and droughts wiped out the water supplies. The winds and freezes destroyed the farms and stopped all food production. Giant migrations started across the continent as people began to search for food and water. Civil order remained in countries like France with nuclear power, and in Russia with its oil and gas reserves. After a short negotiation, the Russian Army took total command of the EU.

In early 2036 the fairness and completeness of news reporting within the NAF began a further slide and then dropped to new lows within four months. A mixture of government controls and failure of infrastructure caused the problems. The cable networks ran into problems getting power to keep their signals on the line, and the government decided to strictly control the news we heard. Agencies started cracking down on the more vocal bloggers.

Abby and I lived a pastoral existence during the next nine months. I worked on my research into hydrocarbon production from every source I could imagine, and Abby did her graduate studies in all the languages she could muster. We just ignored the world around us, though it became more and more apparent that the economy suffered in a deep depression.

On October 5, 2036, the sky fell on my head. I had completed all the course work for my Ph.D. in the middle of the year, passed the qualifying exams, and had begun working on my research and thesis. I expected to have my doctorate completed within nine months.

The head of the Chemical Engineering Department called me into her office and "kindly" informed me that the Federal Government concluded that I possessed a critical skill. They required my presence in Meeker, Colorado, to work on a synthetic fuel project to finish my doctorate. I would not be allowed to finish it if I stayed at Davis. "Here are your orders," she said, handing me a large manila envelope.

I sat there stunned and stammered, "But I don't want to go to Colorado."

She laughed and said with a tone of irony, "In today's world, that is no longer your choice. The federal government activated a small provision of the War Powers Act to place everyone in the country under military control, and they want you in Colorado. The good news is that you can complete your thesis project there. So you will get your degree." She emphasized the word will. "The bad news is that I am going to miss you, son. Good luck." She reached out to shake my hand.

After thinking a moment about the situation, I realized I would find no value in fighting the decision, and I should make the best of it. I returned to our studio and told Abby what happened, and that I wanted her to go with me. Her sweet smile flashed, and she said, "Of course I'm going with you. I'll put the finishing touches on my doctoral thesis tonight, and travel will be no problem for me. How soon do we leave?"

However, her parents objected and pleaded with us to make our marriage official. The awkward moment for me happened when Abby's mother gave me a hug and said, "You understand, of course, Steven and I want so much to become grandparents. You and Abby arrange your schedules and get busy." She smiled at me, and I could see the longing on her face, but I also recognized the futility of bringing a new person into the uncertain world Abby and I found ourselves in.

"We'll see what happens." I hugged her back, and we let the threads of that idea hang.

Abby and I had three weeks to get ready to leave for Colorado.

"End of file Chap-4," said the Puter.

The ProfSir said, "Now we understand that Sam Hardy devoted his higher education to the problem of extracting fuels from the shales of the central continent. I have read interesting reports at the university of this research, and how it ultimately could not provide the energy the society required.

"But we also know that he lived here in the Oregon Lands. His journey to Colorado and back to this place must have been an interesting experience, and we will hear more about it tomorrow evening."

He looked over his group of young archaeologists and added, "Since I have decided to keep our camp at this location in Sutherlin for the next three days, I expect to hear reports of your findings tomorrow evening. Then we will move north to one of our next prospects."

CosandJo lowered his head and closed his eyes. His tingling told him that everything they needed to know could be found here in Sutherlin, near where he had found the memory disks. He just had to find the source of his tingling.

Chapter 5: To Meeker

October 15, 2036

ProfSir ElderJan looked over the group of young archaeologists gathered in the tent. They had worked hard during the day.

"I compliment all of you for the dig today. ShoJan, what did you find?"

The young neophyte held up a rusty disk of iron with a knob at one end. "This looks like it could have been a cooking utensil. But there is little left to see if it had some other use."

ProfSir nodded to the girl. "Our curators can find out much more when they do their analysis at the university." He asked, "CarlJa, you followed the trail to the west. Did you find anything?"

The husky young man stood up from his rug and showed the class several aluminum bars. "These came from the metal deposits I located about three klicks down alongside the creek. I am not sure what they were used for, but there are some large deposits in the area with iron and aluminum minerals. It appears there may have been some kind of storage area there."

The ProfSir took one of the pieces from CarlJa. "Aluminum lasts quite a long time, unlike the iron that rusts quickly. We should take these back with us to Hudson Bay and mark the area where you found the deposits on our maps for future reference. It may be a potential salvage mining site.

"CosandJo, did you find anything more?" the ProfSir asked.

The young man hung his head. "No, ProfSir. I poked into most of the mounds in the area this morning, and I found nothing. There is nothing else here to find." His despondency showed in the droop of his shoulders.

The ProfSir shook his head and said, "CosandJo, you must develop a more positive approach when doing archeology and salvage. There is much to find in this area, but we will need to search more diligently to find it."

Turning to the Puter, he spun the disk in the Magic Reader as he said, "The last time Puter spoke to us, we heard how Sam started his journey to a place called Meeker in Colorado. Now that we have ourselves moved to Sutherlin, we have time to study this area and listen to more of Sam's history."

"But we should have found more," CosandJo said. "There must have been other artifacts from Sam and his tribe. His story may have nothing to do with us."

"Sam's story may not be the answer to our search, CosandJo, but as I said, it may give us a clue of where else to look. At this time, it is the only story from the Great Collapse that we have. Have patience."

The ProfSir continued, "It is time for us to hear the next episode in the saga of Sam Hardy, about his trip to Colorado. Puter, please say to us the file, Chap-5."

As a wedding present Abby's dad gave us an almost new 2034 E-coupe, guaranteed to get at least ninety-eight mpgq (miles per gallon, equivalent—back in those days you expressed the efficiency of your vehicle by how far it would go on an equivalent to one gallon of liquid fossil fuel), with a one-wheeled trailer. We began collecting things we thought we would need in the Colorado wilderness. Abby's mom kept giving us things to take along, like a stroller and baby clothes, and I hid those items we would not use in the attic of their garage. No way would I haul unneeded weight from California to Colorado.

I had been assigned a priority number authorized by the military authorities for the trip so I could purchase fuel, and I would be reimbursed for the move, but it would not cover all the costs. I advertised on the Internet and found another couple, Harold and Theo, who agreed to pay half the fuel cost for a ride to Gillette, Wyoming. Harold told me of the job he had lined up there to work on a coal gasification project; Theo's experience as a cook meant he could land a job in a greasy-spoon once they reached their destination.

Planning for the trip became our major preoccupation. The big problem turned out to be locating fuel sources between Davis and Meeker. The E-car needed hydrogen for the fuel cells, and outside of California, H_2 availability proved to be very limited.

I chose to buy a storage tank that would give me an extra 650 miles over the 250 miles in the car's fuel tank, provided I drove at a slow speed and good sun augmented our supply using power from the solar panels. The Internet said there would be hydrogen fuel service in Reno, Salt Lake City, and in Wyoming at Rock Springs and in Gillette. I already had assurances from the Colorado Syn-Fuel Lab that they could provide hydrogen at the lab in Meeker.

Early on a Monday morning, November 3, Abby and I wished her folks goodbye, and we drove east to cross the Sacramento River to say goodbye to my folks, then up the old Interstate 80 to pick up Harold and Theo in Rocklin. At about 11:00 a.m., we headed east on I-80. The weather forecasts called for heavy rains that night, and it began to cloud over and sprinkle rain. We did not realize how bad it would become.

The potholes on the interstate proved to be worse than what I'd heard they would be, with broken concrete everywhere along the way. We shared the road with several long-haul trucks, but saw very few personal vehicles except for the occasional E-Hummer that screamed past us. We agreed that whoever drove those monsters must either be important government brass or corporate bigwigs. They couldn't be getting more than forty-five mpgq. My dashboard display said my little car averaged at least sixty-eight mpgq, even uphill, and that was loaded with four people and pulling the little trailer.

Years before, Dad took Mom and me up to see the snow above Reno, so I knew something of the route along I-80. However, as we drove into the foothills of the Sierra Nevada Mountains, the dead trees and absence of small bushes and grass on the hillsides amazed me. The effects of the prolonged drought showed everywhere, and the scours from the winter storms had stripped the hillsides and mountains of even more vegetation. Once we neared the summit, we could sometimes see patches of green vegetation in the distance.

Along with the desolate scenery, a horrendous wind blew over the summit, spitting a fine mist that warned of the storm following us to the east. Several times I feared we would be blown off the side of the road. Once we cleared the pass and headed down toward Truckee, I noticed that the wind decreased a bit.

The sun dropped lower behind us, but still lit the scene before us. We could see a blackened wasteland with a few sentinels of burned pines standing in the area from Donner Lake through Truckee. In 2034 the fires had burned across Rose Mountain and beyond our sight to the north and south. Those humongous flames had destroyed everything. We could not see that far, but I knew the blackened forest encircled all of Lake Tahoe. The resort area of

South Tahoe had been destroyed, and the fire had come back up the west side of the lake. Some of the greatest damage occurred along the Pacific Coast Trail.

We stopped in Reno for the night and parked downtown on a side street not far from the railroad and Virginia Street, the main drag. A steady rain reflected the few lights that shined from inside the casinos, where we could hear the sound of people pulling the handles of those old mechanical slot machines. The electronic slots with their video screens became a thing of the past when electricity costs topped forty-five cents per kilowatt-hour. Harold and Theo went to try their luck and came back broke and wet as dogs in the middle of the night. At least two facts of life remained unchanged: people loved to gamble, and they lost doing it.

After a fitful night in the car, we heated a small pot of water over the hydrogen camp stove I had picked up in a yard sale and brewed a spot of tea with raisins and cracked grain cakes for breakfast. Abby pleaded, "Why can't we go into a casino and drink a cup of real coffee?"

Theo answered before I could speak. "Not me. They want seven dollars for a plain cup of coffee. They say it's imported. I'll stick with tea, even if it's made from the local juniper berries."

I drove to the fueling station in Sparks to top off my hydrogen tanks, and we headed east on I-80 toward Salt Lake City. We heard on the radio that a steady downpour pounded the length of California, and spotty rain kept my windshield from drying.

Winds picked up after we left Reno, blowing dust and sand across the road in front of us. Enough rain fell to turn the dust into mud that coated the car, and the wind did not let up for the entire trip. Even though I could not see the road that well, the GPS tracking antenna and steering control continued to function and keep us centered on the highway. Unfortunately, the collision avoidance radar only saw other vehicles, not the potholes and road cracks. Several times I thought the E-car must be falling into a canyon, but it righted itself, and we continued ahead.

After little over an hour, Harold said, "The map shows there's a roadside rest in a couple of miles. We better stop. That tea is about to overflow my system." After I pulled into the rest stop, everyone braved the pelting rain to stretch their legs and relieve their bladders.

Abby grimaced and suggested, "Let's make it a plan to stop every hour at a rest stop or intersection along the way for a potty break. That okay?"

We all nodded in agreement, and I told them, "But let's not stop for food. We can eat in the car as we're moving. Each of us has a water bag, and should have enough to get to Salt Lake City. Let's keep moving."

We drove on, heading northeast through the dust and mist in seventy mile-per-hour winds. We made good time at forty-five miles-per-hour when our route put our backs to the winds, but most of the time we did about thirty-five miles per hour with a hard crosswind.

About noon I asked, "Who wants to drive? I've been at this wheel for four hours now, and my eyes are starting to cross from staring into this dust."

Theo volunteered, and I pulled over to the side of the road. Abby and I moved to the back seat, and I laid my head on her shoulder. Before I dropped off, I warned Harold. "Keep an eye on your driver. You're responsible for seeing that he doesn't pass out."

Harold chuckled, "Yes, boss. I'll poke him in the ribs if his eyes even flutter for a millisecond."

Every four hours we switched drivers. We all felt dirty and dry, but after twenty-seven hours of constant travel under cover of mixed dust and rain, we made it across the salt flats into Salt Lake City.

I took back the driving chores and set the GPS to lead us to the fueling station. The car showed another fifty miles of hydrogen fuel left in storage, and the batteries showed a half charge.

"We fuel official cars, not the public," the attendant said. "Sorry, bud, but just move on."

With a weary smile, I pulled out my orders and held them in front of him. After a moment, he said, "Oh, okay. Guess you're legit, but we get some funny people in here trying to buy fuel. But let's see your money first." Once satisfied, he attached the stainless steel fittings and began to fill my tank. The tank turned a frosty white as the ultra-cold gas evaporated from the super-cooled liquid and entered the tank to be absorbed into the nanosilver mesh.

"Any suggestions of a good place to rest up?" I asked.

He looked at the four of us, all dirty from our time on the road. "You just came in from Reno, didn't you? Well, go south about five miles to the Fruit House. They offer some small rooms for rent and good fresh food. Looks like you all need to recover."

The Great Salt Lake is filled with undrinkable water, but the rivers that flow into the lake are fresh water. Utah always showed concern about water and learned how to manage and conserve water from the beginning. Now, with global warming, other places around the world found they either had too much or too little water. With little experience managing that resource, many areas encountered a difficult time coping with the necessary changes.

Early in the twentieth century, 90 percent of the people in the U.S. lived on the coastlands around our country, but by 2034, with the near one meter rise in sea levels, the country forced massive evacuations from New Orleans, Houston, New York, and any other areas within fifteen feet of sea level as measured in the year 2000. The government now warned that the sea level would continue to rise for the foreseeable future, and no one could offer any valid reason to linger. And when someone moved, they might as well move high enough to be safe for a long time.

The rising tides caused massive destruction of industrial capacity along the coast. Seas inundated many of the U.S. refineries and factories built along the bays and inlets from the oceans, and other industries found it difficult to pick up and move to higher ground. Planners did not anticipate the depletion of the land resources.

A growing shortage of usable water, both for drinking and for farming, became the bigger problem around the country. Cities from coast to coast struggled to find enough water to support their citizens, and in most cases turned to water rationing to get along. Pollution filled many rivers and lakes, making them unusable for drinking or for industry. Places in southern California had built themselves on a water culture, and when it dried up, the culture evaporated and blew away with the dust.

You cannot grow food or make biofuels without water. By 2036 the continued irrigation in Missouri, Iowa, Kansas, Nebraska, and the Dakotas exhausted water from the Ogallala aquifer, and only aquifers around the major riverbeds produced water in the Midwest plains, once called the breadbasket of America. The industrial farms, all owned by large multinational corporations, stole as much water as they could from the surrounding towns and continued to raise grains to feed their ethanol and bio-diesel plants. Clouds of a water war appeared on the horizon.

We rested in Salt Lake City for three days, alternating with two sleeping in the car and two in the rented room. The Fruit House carried fresh local produce, and we gorged ourselves on those delicacies. And their water tasted wonderful. We all found it hard to pull away.

After the trip across the Nevada desert and the salt flats of the Salt Lake, the next leg of our trip felt like a walk in the park. We enjoyed an easy trip into Rock Springs, Wyoming, in one day over a roadway maintained and repaired with fresh gravel.

"Long-hauler coming up behind us. Better pull over." With Theo's warning I looked for a wide spot alongside the gravel highway. The dust blew through everything if you traveled close to another vehicle, so we would stop from time to time to let a long-haul truck speed on past us and wait another five minutes to let the dust settle.

I approached my next fueling stop west of Rock Springs alongside the Green River. I pulled in next to the pump and looked around. "What's happening? The flow in Green River looks stagnant," I asked the attendant at the fueling station.

"Man, we just need some rain. It's been more than nine months since any rain fell, and it's worse back up in the mountains 'cause there ain't been no snow. Down south, the Flaming Gorge Reservoir is less than a tenth full. We need some rain."

Abby returned from their little store empty-handed. "They don't offer much of anything, and the prices are all sky-high. I think we better be satisfied with cheese and crackers tonight." We drove down by the river and found a level spot where we could spread some blankets on the river rocks for the night. It turned cool when it got dark.

The next morning I continued east, then turned off I-80 and headed over the high plains of Wyoming, past Independence Rock where the Oregon and Mormon Trails and the Pony Express passed 180 years before, down into Casper, north on I-25, then northeast on State 387 across the grassy desert toward Gillette. Apart from the rough road and parched dry grass covering the hills, you could not tell a weather problem bothered this land. When you saw no other vehicles on the roads for hours at a time, Wyoming just felt big and lonely.

We reached Gillette in good time and took Harold and Theo to their friend's house. They invited us in for supper, and everyone enjoyed a very convivial time with everyone else. Their small, tight-knit community depended upon everyone watching out for everyone else. Harold and Theo would do fine.

While visiting with Harold's extended family, we caught up with world news on their TV. We had not realized how awful the flooding had become in California. We called back home, but the phone lines did not work. I sent emails to our families asking for status, knowing we could not receive replies until we reached Meeker. Abby and I both worried ourselves sick.

The network news said some politicians in California expressed concerns about the flooding potential around Sacramento and talked about moving to a new capital built on the hills above Palo Alto, near San Jose. I told Theo's friend, "Don't they realize that would put their butts on the San Andreas Fault, or maybe they figure things can't get much worse."

Abby and I left the next morning for Meeker. Our 420-mile route alongside the crest of the Rocky Mountains offered a beautiful drive if you ignored the dead vegetation. We camped a couple of nights on the side of the road. At the top of the 7,500-foot pass just above Meeker, we found some snow on the ground and stopped to play in it. It was the first time Abby had seen snow.

We reached Meeker about noon the first week in December and drove through a quiet, sleepy town. We continued to the SynFuel Combustion Research Laboratory, three miles west of town, and checked in at the gate. They reviewed my papers and assigned us to Barracks R at the lab. Once again we lived in our own home, a one room efficiency apartment.

After unloading the trailer, I accessed the Internet to check on the state of things back in California. After several tries, I got in touch with our parents. It looked bad, with the rains still pouring down across the state. Flooding had started, and a major flood appeared inevitable. We continued to communicate with our parents as things went from bad to worse.

In January it began to snow in California. I warned Dad to get out; a warm rain on top of that snowpack would create havoc. He said he and Mom needed to do a few more things in Sacramento, but they would leave as soon as they could. Then the rains returned the first week in February, and within three days the city of Sacramento disappeared beneath the muddy water. Abby and I watched the disaster unfold on the TV screen. It looked like the end of the world.

"End of file Chap-05," said the Puter.

"As anticipated, that flood destroyed the center of California," said the ProfSir.

CosandJo asked, "How many people did the flooding affect?"

"Some of the historical reports I saw estimated that as many as twenty million people died from the floods and starvation that struck the California regions during and immediately following this period."

The class shook their heads in unison.

Chapter 6: In Meeker

February 2, 2037

"Class, I know you all worked hard today and searched this area for salvage and items of archeological significance, but I also note that you did not find much. CosandJo mentioned his concerns yesterday, Why do you think that would be?"

PaulJa held up his hand and received a nod from the ProfSir. "It looks to me like someone else has already mined the salvage in this area. There are a few caches of materials, but for the most part there is nothing left."

"PaulJa, you are right. Sam Hardy's tribe probably moved here because it was a good area for salvage, and after a few years, they had cleaned it out. The tribe would have needed to move on if catastrophe had not overtaken them. We should keep this lesson in our minds, for even now we have limits to our resources.

"CosandJo, do you think that is the explanation?"

CosandJo looked up with a start. He had been wondering what happened to the tingling he had felt yesterday. "Oh, I suppose that could be, but yesterday morning I felt there should be more, then today I did not have that feeling."

"Interesting," ElderJan said. "I will take your feelings under advisement."

Turning to the Puter, ElderJan spun the disk in the Magic Reader as he said, "The last time Puter spoke to us, we heard how Sam had been instructed to move to Colorado to work on the oil shales project. This next chapter tells of the floods in California and Sam's efforts and life in Colorado."

"Puter, please say to us the next file, Chap-6."

Sacramento disappeared from the face of the earth in February 2037, but it started the previous November, about the time Abby and I left UC Davis on our journey to Colorado.

The weather gurus said the so-called Pineapple Express weather system, a result of an even stronger El Nino weather cycle, had strung out across the Pacific Ocean and focused the tropical jet stream with its load of moisture from the south-central Pacific straight over northern California. Once the rains started, it rained day and night.

By Thanksgiving, rains had drenched the entire northern part of the state, and by early December the flat lands of the Sacramento and San Joaquin valleys lay under a foot of rainwater with nowhere to drain. In the middle of the month, the Sacramento River had breached its levees between Redding and Chico. By the end of the year, all the flood control reservoirs in the foothills were pouring uncontrolled amounts of water over their floodgates, and every river from the Klamath in the north to the Kern in the south gushed out of their banks and filled the lands around them. Farms and cities were covered by the growing lakes spreading from the Sacramento and San Joaquin rivers.

In Davis and Sacramento, the clouds dumped at least an inch of rain every day for seven weeks, sometimes as much as six or seven inches. The grounds in and around Sacramento could not drain the water, and the Sacramento and American rivers rose higher and higher. For a while the levees protecting downtown Sacramento and the capital offices from the American River held firm.

The night before Christmas, the jet stream shifted to blow from the north, and it sucked a column of cold air south from Alaska. The rains stopped, and instead snow began to fall and accumulate in the Sierra Nevada Mountains. With a reprieve, the standing water in the fields dropped, and some levee breaches around the city received the attention they so sorely needed.

Storm after storm plunged down from the Gulf of Alaska, and snowdrifts grew to more than forty feet deep at Donner Summit. In January some of the more hardy skiers returned to the Sierras. People rejoiced that the rains had stopped. They exclaimed that once again Sacramento had defeated its rivers.

I emailed my father to get out while they could. "Leave Sacramento, *now*. If anything goes wrong, it will be a disaster," I said. He made a lame excuse about needing to finish a state project, and besides, "the rain has stopped. Now we just get snow."

In the second week of February, the El Nino pattern pulled the jet stream back south. Another slug of warm moisture flowed in from the central Pacific. Once again, front after front rolled in from the west, crashing into the mountains, and this time warm rains fell to melt the snow. The snow level rose from five thousand feet to nine then ten thousand feet overnight. Rain poured across the mountains, atop the record pack of snow.

It took just over three days for the entire forty-foot snow banks to melt, adding their forty-inches of moisture content to the additional twenty-three inches of rain that fell north and south of Donner Summit, from Shasta to Whitney.

Shasta Reservoir on the Sacramento, Oroville Reservoir on the Feather, and Folsom Lake on the American had remained full from December on, even though they dumped water at flood rates for days. The additional rainfall spilled unchecked over their spillways and poured down the rivers. Marysville and Yuba City disappeared beneath the waters of the Feather and Yuba Rivers, and to the south, Olivehurst, protected by levees built in 2008 declared as impregnable, vanished overnight.

When the Folsom dam breached, water rose thirty feet above flood stage on the American River. Sacramento's levees crumbled within minutes and the worst flood imaginable swept the entire metropolitan area into the Sacramento Sea. From Chico to Modesto, the Sacramento and San Joaquin valleys filled with floodwater trying to push its way through the Carquinez Straits against high tide. Water ran fifteen feet above flood stage through the channel near Martinez.

Floodwaters backed into Davis. We received one email from Abby's parents, telling us how they sat watching the catastrophe from their second-story studio while holding onto each other in the sparse light from their stock of candles and listening on their windup radio to the few radio stations still operating. We never heard from them again.

When the rains stopped ten days later and the waters began to recede, the state listed over one hundred and thirty thousand people as known dead or lost. I never received official word, but I always assumed they counted my Dad and Mom and Mom's parents among those lost in Sacramento, and Abby's parents lost in Davis.

On March 15, 2037, my twenty-second birthday, Abby and I held a private wake for our lost ties to our childhood.

"Puter, please pause here." The ProfSir mopped his brow.

"Class, the California floods of 2037 are described in the university records as among the worst to strike the North American continent, and when I read those reports at the university, they were dry and factual.

"To hear a report from a couple with direct ties to the stricken area is heart wrenching. We must always remember that the earth has its own way of dealing with matters. Sometimes, we humans will be severely tested."

The class sat quietly, waiting for the ProfSir to resume the reading.

"Puter, please continue."

//////// \\\\\\\\

Abby and I picked up our lives and moved on.

At the SynFuel Laboratory in Meeker, Colorado, I did experiments much like what I did as a graduate student at UC Davis, except now I used a real geological formation to work with. I soon found that all the things that went so well in theory did not work so well in fact.

Not so long after I arrived it became apparent, at least to me, that unless someone could make a huge breakthrough, we would use more energy to make a gallon of synfuel than the energy it could deliver. When I pointed this out to my supervisor, he jerked me into his office and slammed the door.

"Dammit, do not, and I repeat, *do not*, say anything like that around here again," he shouted. "The walls have ears, and some people do not like words of discouragement. Remember, our supply of raw material is infinite, so anything extra we can produce here is profit." His logic seemed illogical to me at the time, but I heeded his warning and kept my mouth shut, except for talking to Abby.

Then I had to convince Abby that she should not spread the word out over the Internet. We finally agreed we must live the lie to survive in Meeker.

"Puter, stop again."

The ProfSir said, "Sam is telling us here about the level of denial within the old civilization. The authorities would attack anyone who said that they could not get a supply of fuel from whatever resource they chose."

SamJan asked, "Didn't they understand simple mathematics?"

"Some understood the mathematics, but too often society's initial assumptions were wrong. Their biases were too strong. The ways of the world were too set. It is amazing how much they seemed to be determined on finding ways to destroy themselves."

The class shifted uncomfortably.

The ProfSir said, "Puter, please continue."

Abby and I buried ourselves in our work to blot out those images of California. She took on more students over the Internet to tutor in languages, and kept herself very busy. I focused on putting together the equipment for my experiment in the lab. We both hoped and waited for news from our parents, but all in vain.

The Internet service at the Lab exceeded by far anything Abby and I had ever experienced. I dabbled in the commodities markets, and for the next two years our life was pleasant but uneventful. What with the "free" hydrogen fuel available from the Lab, we lived in the most prosperous community on the planet. The government brought in a group of farmers who grew a marvelous selection of fruits and vegetables in the greenhouses constructed on the lab property.

We settled into the routine of using electrical power from the coal-powered generation plants up in Wyoming to suck liquid fuels from the oil shales in Colorado and send whatever we could to the east.

Abby and I took the opportunity to go on numerous hikes into the mountains and learn more about the country around us. On a jaunt in early spring in 2038, we stopped alongside a tiny stream on the side of a mountain, and Abby asked me, "Sam, do you think we could have a baby? Mom and Daddy wanted us to deliver a grandchild, and I feel so guilty not giving them one."

I sat down on a nearby boulder and buried my head in my hands. I had always feared this subject would come up. I shook my head and talked through my hands. "Abby, however nice it may seem at the lab, this world we live in is hell, and I believe it is going to get worse. What I am working on here is garbage and will never solve the problems facing our world. They are just trying to find a replacement for the gasoline and biofuel the population is using to drive their cars, not find a solution to the energy problem for humanity. Soon there will be even more massive die-offs around the world, including here in our country. I don't believe it would be fair to place anyone into this kind of world, in particular a child of ours. Do you really think we should?"

She stared off into the distance, and I could see tears streaming down her cheeks. "No, you're right. It wouldn't be fair. It would be cruel." She sniffed. "But someday when things get better, I want a baby."

"When things get better, Abby, we will have a baby. I promise." I just could not see any way or any time when I could make things better.

In the middle of the U.S., the Midwest water wars flared across the plains, just on the other side of the mountains east of us. As water wells went dry across Nebraska, Kansas, Oklahoma, and Texas, neighboring farms began to sabotage the irrigation systems of each other, accusing their neighbors of pumping water from beneath their cropland. The few remaining cities that pumped groundwater for their citizens proved to be poor country cousins as the big corporations became more and more aggressive. Soon, gangs of hired thugs roamed the remaining farmlands, wrecking whatever they could find, fighting between themselves in maniacal rage.

In an effort to alleviate the food shortages, the federal government demanded that 40 percent of the corn and soybean crops in the Midwest be allocated to producing cereal staples for the people of the federation. The corporations screamed foul, but with reluctance sold a portion of their crops to the government for use as food stocks. They wanted the larger profits they made from using the grain for biofuels.

The North American Federation outlawed exports of grain to the rest of the world as a food staple, and very few chicken, beef, and pig farms remained.

As the weather patterns continued to warm, northern Canada came online as a major grain source, but most of the production remained with the older farms in the Midwest belt of the old U.S..

Water also became the major problem in southern California. After the devastating floods of 2037, the great water distribution system of California lay in total ruins. The floods finished the creation of the Sacramento Sea that started with the earthquake twenty years earlier in the middle of the state. Water could no longer be taken from the Sacramento delta and shipped to the south to water the giant San Joaquin valley farms and greater metropolitan Los Angeles. Water from the Colorado River that could be shipped to southern California became more and more scarce as that river flowed less and less, and the southern third of California transformed back into the deserts found before 1900.

Without sufficient water, southern California produced little food, and few nearby food sources provided for the region. Often farmers could not find fuel to ship what food they could grow into the Los Angeles basin. Migration rates exploded. Southern Californians packed all they could carry into their cars and trucks, filled their tank from some source of liquid fuel, and headed out, searching for a better land. Over eight million "Calypsos" as they came to be called, most of them poor and destitute, flooded toward the lands east of the Mississippi in a search of a better option. Another two million headed north into the San Joaquin and Sacramento valleys. They joined the indigenous homeless population, dependent upon the government to provide them with food and water.

The smartest of the two million that remained around Los Angeles joined with the criminal gangs and lived a life supported by slaves and extortion. They traded their dope and drugs for fruits and grains from the California valleys to the north. In time, they began to encroach into the valleys, spreading their regimes and gang warfare throughout the refugee camps.

Around the world the situation grew ever direr, with mass migrations everywhere migration was possible. Starving hordes moved from place to place, like clouds of locusts or a march of lemmings, leaving behind a trail of starved bodies and wasted lands. Those not killed by the starvation, heat prostration, and lack of water died from the spreading pandemics.

On July 4, 2038, another disaster struck the North American Federation. The New Madrid Fault in the middle of the continent, under the Mississippi River, fractured with a 7.9 magnitude earthquake, a repeat of the first monster quake in the series that started December 16, 1811. Another 7.4 magnitude earthquake hit just hours later on the thrust portion of the fault near the town of New Madrid.[1]

The earthquake destroyed the two largest cities near the fracture, Memphis, Tennessee, and St. Louis, Missouri. In addition, Louisville, Nashville, Jackson, Shreveport, Little Rock, and Chicago suffered severe damage. Six hundred thousand square miles of the center of the country lay torn by the shaking. The earthquake left almost ten million people homeless or without any kind of support infrastructure. It caused half a million injuries, and

---

1   See *Memphis 7.9 (Revised)* and *Broken River* by Sam Penny at amazon.com for details

tens of thousands of deaths. The effects of the earthquake series proved to be ten times worse than Hurricane Katrina, thirty-four years earlier.

That earthquake broke the back of our country's economy. It cut so many lines of communication and transport that the entire distribution system laid in ruins. The country lost so much infrastructure that it could never recover. Though the damage happened half a thousand miles away, it surprised me how much and how rapidly it affected our lives and the research in Colorado. Within weeks, products from the eastern part of the country vanished from the shelves of the stores and storerooms of the lab. We found spare parts to no longer be readily available. Food staples became scarce. Everything was in short supply. People began to hoard certain items, like toilet paper and salt.

I tried to warn my friends at the lab about the impending crunch on our research and production. At some point we would all suffer from some kind of calamity where a needed part would not be available any longer. But for the most part, no one would listen. They argued that everything would turn out okay in time. A few listened to my suggestion that they should at least think of how to prepare for worsening conditions.

At the lab we continued to produce power from the shales of Colorado, but spare parts became a primary concern. Many critical items we needed came from the east or south coast factories and were no longer accessible. The source might have been destroyed in the shaking, or the factory that made it could no longer get power, or the feedstock it needed dried up. Our suppliers always found some kind of excuse.

I could see the handwriting on the wall. The research department at the SynFuel Lab made less and less progress and enthusiasm dropped lower and lower. Production levels slowed as we got into more difficult geology and the quality of the shale bed fell. I told Abby I believed it to be a matter of time before they pulled the plug, but I could not tell her just what that would mean. She started getting things in order around the home, just in case, and we lived from day to day.

One night in December 2038, the TV displayed scenes from across the country and the rest of the world, and we watched it all in horror. The announcer said, "Based upon food and energy production rates around the world, one estimate from the Carnegie Think Tank is that by 2040 the Earth's "carrying capacity" will drop to less than 60 percent from where it started, to an approximate 3.5 billion. That does not take into account the water scarcity that also developed. Nor does it consider what might be the impact of the giant earthquake in the middle of the country."

One of the commentators on a different show reported, "The estimated world population now stands at 4.6 billion, down from a high of 7.5 billion in 2016. At least 3 billion people died from pandemics or starvation in the past twenty years."

Abby gasped, "That means there will only be enough food and energy in the world to support maybe 3.5 billion people next year. We're still a billion too high."

"That's right. We're in the middle of the great collapse of the human race."

Abby and I agreed that the TV media must feel it their responsibility to show every bit of the tragedy. One of the older commentators said, "Broadcasting today is like what I remember from back in the Vietnam times. It's just too much, too awful."

So we stopped watching television. As 2038 wound to a close, we felt so lost, so old. Still a young couple by some standards, twenty-one and twenty-three years old, our world ended before we could experience it.

Puter said, "End of file Chap-6."

The Profsir drew in a breath, then exhaled a loud sigh. "Life turned terrible to those who saw their world falling apart. So many people died, and in the end, so few survived." He looked over the class. "We must understand how and why they survived, but first we must understand from where they came. What motivated them? What made Sam Hardy willing to keep trying?"

CosandJo looked down into his hands, shaking his head. He too wondered, *"Why? What could keep anyone going in that kind of world?"*

ProfSir ElderJan cleared his throat. "Class, I have decided we must start our journey back to the north to return home before the weather becomes too fearsome. Prepare to move tomorrow morning. We will journey north to Ugene and camp on the banks of the Wilimet River."

Chapter 7: Failed Dream

December 31, 2038

ProfSir ElderJan and his troop made good time traveling north from Sutherlin. They moved past the area they knew as Ugene Town and camped on the west side of a large river shown on their maps as the Wilimet.

After a quick supper, the students gathered in the big tent with ProfSir ElderJan.

CosandJo asked, "ProfSir, why did the people of 2040 abandon their efforts to find more fuel for their civilization?"

The ProfSir coughed, then said, "CosandJo, much of the effort to find fuel was to support their transportation system. But by that time the cost of finding and producing petroleum had grown to the point that petroleum effectively became unavailable to those who needed it the most. Everyone looked for a good replacement. But they did not start soon enough on the development of renewable fuels or alternative means of transportation, so they never produced enough to supply the whole populace.

"But the best way to understand is to hear it from someone who lived in that time. Let's let Sam Hardy tell in his own words why they gave up their search.

"Puter, please say to us the next file, Chap-7," said ProfSir ElderJan.

As we were getting ready for the SynFuel Lab's 2039 New Year's Eve cel-ebration, I told my wife, "Honey, our time here in Meeker is about over."

"What do you mean? Did you hear something at the lab?" Abby rubbed the polished worry stone I gave her at Christmas and looked at me with a troubled expression. The stone worked half-way. It relieved her strain but did not relieve the worry.

I stirred the cup of sage tea that finished my dinner and looked up. "I've been talking with some other guys at work, and everyone is concerned that the government is about to end research here at the SynFuel Lab, and maybe even the production facility itself will close."

"But why would they do that?" she asked.

"My Conversion Project needs some special control parts from an electron-ics outfit in Tennessee. It's been almost six months since the New Madrid fault fractured, and yesterday is the first time I got through on the phone to talk with their chief engineer. He said that the earthquake messed up their plant and everything else in Nashville, and they're still trying to put things back together. He said they'd ship more components to me as soon as they could, but he wouldn't give me a date.

"Worse than that, last time I checked, the transport lanes across the Missis-sippi from Tennessee are still mostly closed, so even if he can produce the parts, I may not be able to receive them. It doesn't sound promising."

"Haven't you been able to find the parts somewhere else?"

"The other source that made the type of controls I need was in southern California, and that's a wasteland now." I paused and looked out the window of our small barracks apartment at the blowing snow and dust, a common feature around Meeker. "No, this place can't keep going, and I think we'd better prepare a way to get out."

Abby stared at me for a moment, shrugged her shoulders, and then asked in her usual matter-of-fact way, "Okay, so what do we do?"

I breathed a sigh of relief. My worry that Abby would go into denial when I told her of my concerns had been unfounded. I was pleased to see she took it like a trooper. "Well, I talked to this mechanic I met in town about trading our E-car for an ancient motor home belonging to an old woman he knows. It's been modified for electric drive. She has kept it in her barn all these years and it's in perfect condition. It's twenty-two feet long, but it would sleep the two of us and includes facilities for cooking and indoor plumbing. We could go most anywhere with it."

Abby put her hand to her mouth and raised her eyebrows. Then she smiled and said, "I remember how motor homes went out of style as I grew up. We thought everyone who drove them must be greedy fools."

"Yeah, most of those old buses and trailers got parked or junked. But this baby has been stored in a barn just outside of town for almost thirty years, so it's still in good shape, except all the rubber has dried up. All I have to do is requisition some tubing and a set of solid tires for it from the lab."

"So where do we get fuel for this thing, and how much are you talking about paying for it?"

"The electric generator in the coach is already flex fuel. It'll run on synfuel, ethanol, gasoline, or diesel. The roof is covered with solar panels, and I found an electric hydrolysis H_2 generator I can buy cheap, so we can generate a good supply of gas. We can use the H_2 storage tank we brought with us on the trip here, and I know where I can get a fuel cell to make the electricity for the drive so we can get some distance out of the sun if we run out of liquid fuel. If it turns cloudy, at least we'll get enough power to use our in-house appliances."

"How much?"

I coughed. "I can get the motor home and the parts I am talking about, whole shebang, for just under a million. And my Australian gold account holds that much. I know it's a lot, but I think it's good insurance."

She leaned her head to one side and frowned. "Okay, that gold isn't doing us much good where it is, and you'd do it anyway. But I agree with you. We need a way out." She smiled again and rubbed the worry-stone into the palm of my hand. "So where are we going to go?"

"Back to California. It still offers most of the natural resources that we need."

"Do you still want to celebrate New Year's Eve? This sort of changes things."

"Sure, let's go to the party, but keep your eyes and ears open. Maybe we will find some recruits to go with us." We talked with several of our friends at the party about finding a way out, but without success. Even in times of despair, the known is less threatening than the unknown.

The beginnings of 2039 did not find the world a happy or safe place. Police and army units around the world tried to control society, but as the social protests increased the desertion rates from those services rose too high, and they could not keep up. Rebellions swept the third-world countries and some industrial areas in the North American Federation, and mobs searched out everyone with signs of food, water, or wealth.

Politicians and the elite became prime targets. In particular those who rumor said did not try to save their country were at the most risk. In California they estimated that over half of the people along the coast and in its valleys died of non-natural causes during the 2030s.

Abby and I made repeated attempts to communicate by phone and email with our friends in California. At last I made contact with an enclave at the

University in Davis, holed up in the engineering building after they established a satellite link with the Internet.

Bob, the fellow on the VOIP link told me, "There are mobs roaming the campus, and I don't see much hope that any of us here in engineering can survive. Everything left of central Sacramento has been burned to the ground, and now everyone's gathering here. All the homes in Davis were trashed by the mobs searching for food. The world is crazy. Our hope is that the flu that's spreading around will kill the mobs off before they kill us."

After two days of talking and emailing off and on, Bob never came back on the air.

The Director of the SynFuels Lab in Meeker reported in one of his staff meetings that the government reported the kill-off in Africa and South America to be even more severe than in the NAF, with several countries in the sub-Sahara losing as much as 98 percent of their urban population to starvation and pandemics.

At the lab our high steel fences with razor wire across the top, supplemented by a company of Marines, protected us. Our internal sources for power and water along with hothouses to grow our food sustained us. Best of all, with Meeker located in a backwater area, and a town of three thousand that remained loyal and dependent on us, we remained out of the path of the worst destruction. We had no large population centers of malcontents to provide the mobs that destroyed so much of civilization elsewhere.

However, we still lived on an emotional razor's edge. One of the brighter grad students at the lab made a crack one day in the food hall that humans at last found a way to solve the population problem. He said, "We'll just have food fights and kill each other off," and began to laugh. Another worker in the hall who had received an email that morning about how a mob slaughtered his family in Denver went berserk, grabbed a butcher knife, and before any of the rest of us could stop him, slashed the youngster's throat. This sobering experience demonstrated just how close to insanity each of us lived.

It was in mid-February that a critical pump in the production plant self-destructed. With no parts to fix it, they shut down the big synthetic fuels cracking tower and the main liquids supply column. Without that column, the plant ran at 20 percent of capacity, not enough to feed the lab, much less the town, and definitely not enough to pump down the pipeline to New Orleans.

The next week the director called everyone into the auditorium and told us that he received word from the government headquarters in Atlanta that official work at the oil shale project had ended. The director told the group, "I explained to them that we could not continue without a pump replacement, and the lab could not repair enough furnaces and turbines to continue doing research. Our system is too complex to bring back online. The head man said then that's it—that's the end."

Stunned, everyone sat in silence. The director wiped his eyes and said, "So, you should all prepare to depart this facility at your earliest convenience. The Marines will leave six weeks from now at the end of March."

As the director left the meeting, he beckoned for me to follow him into his office. "Please close the door, Sam. Take a seat."

I did his bidding and sat down on the hard wooden chair, feeling a chill run up my spine. Something else must be wrong.

He opened a drawer in his desk and pulled out a rolled piece of parchment tied with a yellow ribbon and handed it to me. "Here."

"What's this?" I asked as I reached across the desk to take the offering.

"That's your Ph. D. certificate, or at least the piece of paper that says you earned the right to be called doctor," he said. "I've kept it in my desk drawer for the last six months because I wanted you to continue your research. You were the closest to finding the break-through we needed. You gave us your time here, and UC Davis promised you a Ph. D. in return. I'm happy to give you a diploma that says you are Dr. Samuel Julian Hardy, Ph. D., with all rights and privileges in the field of HydroCarbon Synthesis Chemical Engineering."

He gave me a tired smile. "Sam, you did your best here, but it didn't come to anything in the end. We have created too complex a world that cannot stand on its own. I want to thank you for all your work. You are a good kid, and if we lived in the real world, I could say that I expect you to go far."

I stood and felt pleased and angry at the same time. "Thank you, sir. I did my best."

"I know you did. You and many others did their best, but in the beginning we just had too many naysayers who told the world not to worry. Their denial and misplaced optimism got us into this mess. When I was a young man your age, I worked with a group who saw this day coming, but we didn't do much of anything about it. The signs of global warming and the energy and water crunch stood out there like a sore thumb in front of everybody's eyes, but no one wanted to give up their comfortable life and big car and great perks, so we just ignored it. Too many denied that a shortage of fuel amounted to a problem. Now you young folks must live with what my generation let happen. I figure at the very least, we owe you that Ph.D."

His eyes clouded, and his face twisted in agony like he wanted to cry. "Now get out of here."

I turned on my heel and left his office. The next morning he shot himself. I felt sad but relieved for him. He had found his own solution.

Members of my working group discussed boarding up in the lab and staying as long as they could. Abby and I held several long talks with everyone about that approach, and I told them that left them in a hole. They would be depending upon the energy from the lab—if something more quit working, they would be lost. They should come with us.

I talked of my readings about sustainable communities and the need to be able to obtain water and raise food. But they argued that to move from where they felt safe could be too difficult. They wanted to keep everything they had.

Abby and I returned to our apartment and worked on our plans for going back to California. We could not be sure what we would find, but it seemed better than staying in the dry wastelands of western Colorado. We planned how we would search out a sustainable community and join it. We even put together a resume of what we could contribute and posted it on the Internet.

Over the next few weeks, I put in sixteen hour days working on the motor home, getting everything in order for a long trip. I installed the H_2 generator and made sure it could generate hydrogen gas using the solar panels. In the end, I added four more panels to the roof—they stuck out over the side, but I didn't care. I wanted power, not beauty. I located a couple more fuel cells at the lab and confiscated them. One I put into operation and ensured it would generate the electrical power needed to move the rig. The other I tied to the back of the motor home as a backup.

I also confiscated a couple of small hand-operated sump pumps that could be used to suck liquid from a well or underground tank. These turned out to be very important additions to our tool set.

Several years earlier plastics had become a rare commodity, but Abby traded for a collection of plastic containers that we could use to carry water. We also traded for a reverse osmosis water system we could use to make water for drinking and for hydrolysis. I found an old tripod satellite link for TV and Internet and traded a computer for it. Making arrangements to pay for the satellite services proved quite a hassle, but I used the official account of the lab and at last we made it through the red tape. I signed up for ten years of service. I still shielded some of my profits from the carbon trading days stashed away in another account in Canada, and those helped to grease some skids.

Abby also stowed our hoard of grains and beans into the motor home. I knew she collected things but did not realize how much she squirreled away over our months in Meeker.

Reports from the outside world told of growing chaos, and I worried more and more about our safety. Abby and I purchased two handguns, a rifle, and a shotgun from a second-hand dealer in Meeker, and we both practiced and became proficient in their use. I bought several cases of ammunition on the black market, and we stashed the guns and ammo into various crannies in our travel rig.

For practice, I went out with a couple of other guys to do some hunting around Meeker. I even killed an antelope at one point. It provided our group with meat for a couple of weeks, but it tasted pretty raunchy because I no longer ate much meat.

Abby and I worked on finding a destination for our trip. A group in the foothills above Marysville, California, responded to our Internet posting and invited us to join them at a place called Lake of the Springs. They said they lived in an out-of-the-way enclave in the foothills, big in self-sustaining farming, and offered a reliable water supply. I checked it out on Google Maps. It looked and sounded good. We said we would check them out when we arrived in their area in early autumn.

We discussed traveling a route north from Meeker, but that would take us through the Salt Lake City area. After the riots and urban unrest shown on TV over the past two years, we decided we did not want to travel anywhere near a major metropolitan area. Instead, we worked out a route that dropped south to Interstate 70 and then went west to the old Highway 50. We would have to go through Reno to get to the Sierra Nevada Mountains and down to Lake of the Springs, but we remembered Reno as a middle-sized town, not like Salt Lake. It all looked good on the mapping program.

Finally, in the middle of April the weather looked settled. With everything ready, we pitched a big farewell party with our friends at the lab and left Meeker the next morning. We had thought the trip coming to Meeker was a great adventure, but now we started on what would be the trip of our lifetime.

"End of file Chap-07," the Puter said.

The ProfSir said, "Sam has explained to us how the attempts to find alternative energy supplies using shale oil were doomed from the beginning. They used more energy to produce their product than the energy of the fuel they produced. The complexity of their systems raised the risk of failure, and finally, the probabilities caught up with them. They did not keep things simple."

CosandJo asked, "ProfSir, is our society doing that now?"

ElderJan paused, then said, "I have seen a desire in our tribal leaders to move in that direction. They want to grow and expand our reach. Even though they all have a totally rational view of the world we have created, they want more. I sometimes fear they may over-reach.

"That is one of the reasons why neo-archeology and the study of those who preceded us is so important, for there is much to learn about how to live sustainably on the world from those who were forced to do so."

SamJan said, "But Sam made great use of transport himself. He procured this motorhome thing to take he and his wife back to California. That is even farther than we have traveled with our three-wheeled carts on this expedition. Didn't he understand that using fuel for transport was a waste?"

ElderJan smiled. "I am glad you caught the incongruity of this situation. Sam lived in the middle of the collapse of energy resources for the human race, and yet he planned on using whatever energy he could get to move across the country. He still had the thought patterns of the people of that time that transportation was almost a right, and people could go wherever they wanted, if they could just find the fuel to take them there."

PaulJa said, "But I presume that as the fuels became unavailable, his thought patterns became obsolete, and he began to learn how to adjust his travel to his energy budget."

"You are exactly right," said ElderJan. "We are hearing of a transition phase when the human population in the world is shrinking and the foundations for what will follow are being laid. Sam's journeys are not over, even after this next trip from Colorado to California, for we know that in time he came back to Sutherlin here in the Oregon Lands."

CosandJo interjected, "And somehow, he and his family must have formed the roots of our tribe. They have all the characteristics to be our ancestors."

The ProfSir shook his head in exasperation. "CosandJo, you obsess on finding the roots of our tribe. Maybe we will, and the disks you have found may be the evidence we need to prove that, but we must have more to know for sure. This tale we hear from Sam gives us much to study. Be patient. Be patient."

He turned to the rest of the assemblage. "Tomorrow we will hear more about the travels of Sam and Abby from Colorado to California, but remember, class, we must continue our own journey tomorrow as well, so be prepared for an early departure." The ProfSir rose and left the tent.

Chapter 8: Into Nevada

April 4, 2039

The troop of archeologists rose early and continued their journey north along the west side of the Wilimit River. When they could find them, they followed the eroded traces of the old roads in the plains of the Oregon Lands. Those traces were identified by their gravelly base and a noticeable absence of some kinds of weeds.

The path of the troop took them through a mostly flat expanse of grasses dotted with a few trees. In the distance they could see mountains with trees that bordered the valley up which they traveled.

Sometimes they saw mounds of the remnants of the old civilization that existed a thousand years before. Most mounds appeared to be decayed concrete, broken down over the millennium by the weather into piles of gravel and sand. An occasional steel bar appeared from the surface of the mound. The ProfSir had told them that larger buildings from the old civilization were often made using concrete, but it did not withstand the elements very well.

The weather stayed mild but the air became more and more dry. The winds would soon begin to blow in earnest and they expected dust would again fill the air.

Upon reaching the shelter of the hills bordering the western side of the wide valley, they pitched their camp and prepared their evening meal. The ProfSir stroked his chin. "Thank you all for your strong efforts on our trip north. I feel a change coming in the weather, and we do need to move quickly toward our home base in Hudson Bay. It is still a long way from here.

"But in the meantime, as soon as you have eaten we can continue to hear Sam Hardy's story. Today we will hear how Sam and his wife started across the Nevada desert. It is an interesting tale of how our ancestors accepted the concept of powered travel. But this trip took place about the time that concept died, for there were no more supplies of fuel to replenish what they had used."

After the meal ProfSir ElderJan said, "Puter, please say to us the next file, Chap-8."

We began our journey back to California in the antique motor home. It seemed surreal at the time to be stepping away from the edge of the civilized world into what others described to us as a desert ocean, hoping to find another civilization far to the west, almost like Columbus.

When my wife and I left the SynFuel Labs, we headed on a path that would take us across the middle of Utah and Nevada, a land of drought and dry mountains and lakes, now, according to many news reports, devoid of human habitation. We chose as our destination a place in the western foothills of the Sierra Nevada Mountains called Lake of the Springs.

The first leg of our trip required that we drive south to reach Interstate 70, the long-hauler route west out of Denver into Utah. That trip south proved to be easy and offered a chance to see how the motor home, now christened Big Bertha, handled State Route 2039 with its broken surfaces of asphalt, concrete, and gravel. We met no one, and by comparison to later, this uneventful trip could be rated a success as a learning experience.

However, heading west on the Interstate out of Rifle through the Colorado River canyon became a test of my driving nerve—I'm not sure if skill mattered. I had no time to make an evaluation. I most often had less than a second to decide which side I should choose as I approached each obstacle on the almost impassable roadbed, and having made the commitment, drive on. Abby told me at some places where we took some rough detours to get around washouts, she closed her eyes in disbelief that we could make it.

In fact, the trip did not prove all that bad. The long-haul trucks still drove through, so I pushed Bertha into the line and followed along, making it through as well as the truckers. They seemed to enjoy having a fool in their midst.

Upon reaching the "metropolis" of Grand Junction, we found diesel fuel and ethanol to be no problem, but we heard that it would become scarcer as we headed on west. "There should be some kind of diesel at the Green River crossing in Utah," the operator at the Petro Station told me. "If it's not in stock, just wait. It should get there in a couple of days. The government requires that the oil companies keep supplying fuel to the remote fueling stops for the long-haulers."

On the other hand, food shortages plagued the area. We carried a good supply of dried beans and dried antelope jerky from Meeker, but Abby still wanted to stock up on whatever she could find. We found a great hoard of peppers and pepper seeds, commodities that later proved valuable, and she traded much of the antelope for the peppers.

Waving adieu to the Colorado River at Grand Junction, we drove across the mesa country of Utah to the Green River crossing. The Interstate suffered from the beating from the heavy trucks, and with no real maintenance for the past ten years, cracks and potholes covered the majority of the roadbed, even on the level stretches.

At Green River one of the truckers told me, "We used to take the shortcut along Highway 50 to Reno, but that ended two years ago when the flu pandemic swept through the area. No one will drive the fuel trucks into the area, and without fuel, us long-haulers couldn't make it to Reno. Now we head up north and go through Salt Lake City and west along Interstate 80. But that is a tough route, and we carry a shotgun guard. If I was you, I wouldn't go up there—there's too many hoodlums and bandits looking for small game like you."

Abby and I talked about taking the Highway 50 shortcut and depending on Big Bertha's alternate fuels approach to carry us through. Besides, without the big truck traffic, maybe the roads would be better. That is called wishful thinking.

Since this would be the last major water source along our route, we emptied then refilled our water tanks and all our extra water containers using our reverse osmosis water system and checked that all our other systems remained at status go for the long trip across the middle of Utah and Nevada. I rechecked the solar panels and batteries to make sure they showed a solid reserve of electrical power before continuing west.

Once we turned off onto U.S. 50, the roadbed showed its age, but I appreciated that its asphalt crumbled into pebbles, unlike the broken concrete blocks of the Interstate. The government had limited the weight of long-haulers along the U.S. 50 route years earlier to save fuel.

We took our time as we traveled along the remains of the old U.S. 50 and avoided people as much as we could. That proved to be pretty easy since not many people lived near the highway anymore. The locals left or pulled back into their homesteads and showed little inclination to interact with the few of us who traveled on the roads. Whenever we saw someone else on the road, we assumed they must be some kind of officials or bandits and reacted as such. As a result, we acknowledged very few of the people who we did see.

The satellite Internet communications link and satellite TV made a big difference to our life. A good community of people like us continued to use the Internet and offered lots of advice, and we all kept up on the happenings around the world.

We heard news that the ocean fishing stocks failed worldwide and the fishing fleets moved into dry-dock. They still farmed fish, but now they could find little to feed their fish. This added to the problems of worldwide starvation.

We heard news of a new pandemic spreading around the globe. It acted like flu but seemed much more lethal. Without the large amount of worldwide travel as before, it spread at a slower pace from city to city, but it infected everyone and few survived. No medical resources remained to develop a vaccine. I monitored the infection map and did not see it coming anywhere close to our route, so I just made a note to watch its course and put the issue on the back burner.

We crossed the dry lake at Delta, Utah, and continued toward the mountains into Nevada. Upon reaching Ely we saw very few people walking about. I topped off my diesel fuel and stopped by the sheriff's department to ask about the road ahead of us.

The deputy leaned back in his old wooden chair and placed a boot on the bottom drawer. "Son," he said. "I would not advise you to travel that way. In fact, I strongly advise against it. We had a flu epidemic through central Nevada two years ago that wiped out all the towns along U.S. 50. Any law-abiding residents who survived left the county and headed to Salt Lake City, hoping they could find food and medical attention. Anybody that's left out there, I consider an outlaw."

"Do you know of any places where they grew food?" I asked.

"Not really. Back in Delta where you came from, they raise some dairy cattle, but central Nevada went to ranching cattle and mining. Not enough water left for farming, especially not with this drought. There ain't any water out there at all. You really ought to stay here in Ely. We need people like you." He looked me over and seemed pleased about something. Still weighing about 220, I must have looked like a good hefty worker in my scruffy clothes.

I thanked him and went back to our rig to tell Abby what the deputy said. "I think the deputy is looking for a fresh work hand, and he believes I'm it. As far as the towns west of here, those who left could not have drained all the fuel tanks, so I'll check for whatever I can find to fill our tanks. It just sounds like we may get awful lonesome."

Abby nodded. "I heard back when I was a kid that's what they called U.S. Highway 50—the Loneliest Road in the World."

At 3:00 a.m. I switched on our electric motors, and using our batteries, rolled out of Ely making a minimum of noise. I feared the deputy might try to stop us, and I didn't want to offer him an easy chance.

I drove at a slow speed along the rough road, now broken into small pieces of asphalt and gravel. In the rear-view mirrors, I watched the sun come up over the mountains back at Ruth as we reached the top of the Robinson summit, the first pass after Ely. I figured once we disappeared out-of-sight, we would be out-of-mind from the deputy, so after a couple of miles downhill, I found a wide spot at the side of the road, and we stopped for breakfast.

One of my courses at UC Davis taught me about the geology of Nevada. Its interior is a series of small mountain ranges trending northeast, separated by long alluvial valleys. They called it Basin and Range geology. Ely nestled atop the first range, and we had just cleared the second. Over a dozen remained ahead. Our uneventful trip continued on to Little Antelope Summit, Pancake Summit, Pinto Summit, and finally over a pass and down into Eureka.

Eureka began as one of the boomtowns of Nevada, and its mines yielded a significant supply of silver and gold. When the mines gave out, the town became the headquarters for several cattle ranches working on the surrounding hills and down into the valleys.

I stopped beside the road amongst the old mine tailings so we could look down at the remains of the little city.

"What do you see?" I asked.

"What are you looking for?"

"I want to know if there is any sign of life. Do any of the buildings look like they are occupied or being used for anything? To someone out there, our rig and its contents might just be their next bonanza. The deputy said he considered anyone west of Ely to be an outlaw. I agree—guilty until proven innocent."

After ten minutes of observation and seeing nothing, Abby went back to fix a snack while I continued to scan the streets with my binoculars. Then I saw movement. A dog wandered across the street, a pot-bellied, spotted liver-colored hound, maybe fifteen inches tall, her teats hanging heavy under her belly. She sniffed along the side of the road, then came to a stop, staring straight at a clump of weeds ahead. She moved ever-so-slowly forward, holding a rigid point, step by step.

All of a sudden, a cottontail rabbit leapt from beneath the weeds and bounded up the street. The dog dashed ahead to grab the rabbit before it could find a new shelter, and shaking the prey in its mouth, snapped the rabbit's neck. She looked around to see if an audience was watching, then lay down on the street to begin work on the fresh kill.

"Do you like dogs?" I called to Abby.

"Sure, why?"

I restarted the engine and began a slow roll down the street. "Because I think maybe we'll adopt one, one that knows how to feed herself."

The bitch finished off her meal after I stopped on the side of the street opposite her. When she stood up, I could see that her pot-belly and full milk-bags indicated that she would soon birth a litter of pups. I expressed second thoughts about bringing her aboard, but when Abby took a good look at the dog, she turned to me and smiled. "Oh, she will be such great company," she said. Opening the door to the motor home and jumping to the pavement, she called to the dog, "Hello, Hilda, do you want to come aboard Big Bertha?"

The dog walked over to Abby's outstretched hand, sniffed it all around, and then pushed her head under the outstretched palm, asking for a scratch behind the ears. Abby obliged, and the dog wagged her tail, content to once again be in the company of a canine-lover.

"Come on," Abby said as she returned to the motor home. "Sam, her name is Hilda. That was the name of my nanny." Hilda sniffed the stairs and then climbed into the coach. She seemed very content to join our troop and sat down in the middle of the motor home as if she owned it.

I pulled the rig into a fueling station, belted on one of our handguns, and began my search of the area. No one remained in the town, at least as far as I could tell. I determined some fuel remained in one of the underground tanks, and brought out my little sump pump to transfer as much as I could to my tanks.

I entered a couple of rooms, where I found the remains of people who died in bed. Their bodies had become mummified skeletons, with old clothing now draped over the remains. I found no one alive, or any evidence of any-one active in the area.

That night Abby and I locked our doors and went to bed. The sound of Hilda scratching at the covers we put on the floor for her awakened us in the middle of the night. Abby got up and found the bitch in labor and birthing her pups. I went back to bed, but Abby stayed with her and helped. I awoke the next morning to see Hilda lying on the floor with five small puppies struggling to find the best teat. The power of life is strong, and it continued under all conditions.

We left Eureka mid-day and continued on through Devil's Gate toward Austin summit, the next little range.

East of Austin, as we came down the slope into the valley between the mountain ranges, I heard a pop sound from beneath our motor home. It did not sound right, and I stopped to get out and take a look.

"Abby," I called. "Come out here. We've got a problem." There, beneath the engine of the travel rig, I could see a growing puddle of dark liquid.

"Oh my," she said as she stepped to the ground and peered under the coach. "Do you have any idea what that is?"

I reached under the side of the rig, dipped my finger in the puddle, and held it to my nose. "Smells like transmission fluid. That's one thing I didn't plan for." I reached over and took Abby in my arms. "Look around. Here we are on the side of a nice big mountain above a dry wasteland below. This will be our home for a while."

She buried her face into my shoulder and shuddered, then stepped back and smiled through the streaks on her cheeks. "Well, Sam, you've fixed worst things than this. Let's get started."

"Let's do first things first. You fix us something for lunch while I put chocks under the wheels," I replied and smiled.

Later in the afternoon, I let the rig roll down the hill a quarter mile to a flatter spot beside the road where I could climb under the vehicle to check the damage. It did not take long to find a ruptured transmission line, split along the length of the rubber hose. I could close the rupture with my hand, and by wrapping the line with tape, I could affect at least a temporary repair.

"Tomorrow, we'll go into town to look for a replacement hose—I think that has a small chance—and find some transmission fluid—which should be a good chance."

Abby smiled wanly, "Great. Please be lucky. I don't want to spend the rest of my life on the side of this mountain." She reached down to rub Hilda's head.

I took the time to set up our satellite Internet connection on the tripod so Abby could do some surfing. "See anything on the Internet?"

After half an hour, she shook her head, "No, things are just as bad as the last time I looked. I did post notice of our problem here, but no one's made any suggestions yet."

The next morning Abby and I walked down the hill toward town. The motor home rested about a mile-and-a-half up the hill from the center of the small town of Austin. I checked at the fuel station and found a barrel of diesel in the back of the shop. We saw no one or any evidence that anyone remained in the town.

I broke the lock to get inside the mechanics shop at the fueling station. I moved to the back of the building and found the storeroom. Sure enough, resting on the shelf I spied a case of transmission fluid. How lucky could we get? I even found a handcart and a length of rubber hydraulic hose, so I loaded the cart with hose and the cans of fluid, and we moved it all back to our rig.

After replacing the hose, I refilled the transmission, started the engine and let it run for a while in neutral, and topped off the transmission fluid. I prayed when I dropped into first gear, hoping the line would hold. It worked, and I drove down to the center of town. I wanted to be near the place where we could find more supplies.

We wandered around town looking for anyone. We shouted loud at times, but only faint echoes returned. We found more skeletal remains in a few places, indicating that some kind of pandemic must have swept through the area like back in Eureka. Rarely the bodies appeared disturbed. Few scavengers remained to pick over the remains.

The entire town appeared to be abandoned, so we decided to stay around a few weeks. We were nestled amidst a treasure of supplies, and I wanted to choose what to take with us with care.

"What do you think? Should we just stay here for the winter?" I asked.

Abby wrapped her arms around her shoulders. The wind blew cool from the west. "No, I'm afraid this would just be too cold. According to the mapping program, we are at a 6,800 feet of elevation. Don't you think we could freeze?"

One thing about living in a world without much power: there is little energy left over for heating. "Yes, we will move on," I said.

Puter said, "End of file Chap-8."

CosandJo said, "You said it was the end of powered travel, for there was no one to replenish the fuel they used. Did they empty all the fuel tanks?"

ElderJan replied, "No, but Sam and Abby were using the last dregs that remained along that road. However, once those supplies were gone, nothing could use them again."

PaulJa commented, "And it was not just the fuel supplies. Sam was very lucky that he could find the necessary salvage to fix his vehicle. Supplies like that were few and far between."

The ProfSir nodded and said, "And you all know how carefully we planned this trip to be sure we had everything we would need with us. Travel can indeed be a risky venture."

Chapter 9: Cousins

May 5, 2039

The next day the troop packed and moved north from Ugene about fifty klicks to an area marked on their maps with the name of Alban. They passed over a flat land with some indications of former roads and canals. Once filled with farms, now very little water flowed to keep things growing. They made note of a few mounds where remains of the past civilization could be found—possible sources for salvage. After the day of travel and an initial search through the Alban remains, the troop gathered in the big tent for their daily meal and discussion.

ProfSir commented, "You did well getting our camp moved to Alban. Tomorrow we will continue north to the Salem mounds where there should be more archeological remains for us to study. I hope to spend two days at that site if the weather holds."

The ProfSir shifted on his cushion. "SueJa, show us what you found today."

SueJa stood and held a palm-sized rounded silver-colored box in her hand. She turned it over and around for the class to see. Then she put it down and pressed on its side.

She said, "When searching around the mounds near the center of Alban, I discovered something that has lasted over one thousand years and still functions. It is a box in what must be a titanium case that makes music, and it must be solar and nuclear powered, for it still works, and it has touch and voice controls. It produces music from a selection of nearly ten thousand albums stored in its memory, according to its display. I will show you how it works."

Pressing on the side a second time, she said, "Play song" in a commanding voice. After a moment, sound came from the box, and the words "we are the world" could be heard, along with a melodic tune. The class showed their awe: it was unlike anything they ever heard before.

"Stop," she said, and the sound ceased. "I must learn much more about this box of music, and in time we will be able to learn just what kind of music the world experienced before and during the Great Collapse."

ProfSir ElderJan said, "Thank you, SueJan. Class, this is the kind of technology we sometimes find in our searches through the remains of the past civilization. We do not always know how it works, but with research we can learn from it. We may not be able to replicate the technology, but when we find artifacts we can at least see what has been possible in the past."

The ProfSir cleared his throat, coughing away the dust that blew through the tent. "Tonight we will hear more of how Sam and Abby made their journey out of western Colorado after his failed attempt to produce synthetic fuel from the coal beds. And along the way, he finds more of his family. Puter, please say to us the next file, Chap-9."

I always wanted to be a cowboy gunslinger. Some of those old movies I watched as a kid offered great training for the job. But the first time I sat on a horse trying to act like a gunslinger, I realized that I had maybe made the wrong choice.

I should explain. Over a rise to the south of Austin, we found three gaunt horses in a fenced pasture; a young stallion and a couple of mares. In the field next to the horses, resting in the shade of a dead tree, were a pair of donkeys; a jack and a jenny. The windmill supplying their water had pumped dry in the last day or so, and the animals had already picked the grass in the pasture clean. We opened the gates and led them to water on a nearby farm and found some grain and hay. Within a few days, they recovered from their close brush with death and thought of us as their saviors.

Abby located a couple of saddles and some harness in one of the barns, and I found a serviceable wagon in another. I scanned the Internet on how to repair a harness. After a few attempts and trial and error, I learned how to hook horses up to a wagon and worked with the mares so they understood how to pull their load in concert. The stallion would not stand still for the harness, so the mares did all the work. I broke the stallion to a saddle so I could ride him.

We began to pick up things from around town to take along with us. Abby found an old peddle sewing machine and fell in love with it. I found five handguns and three rifles, along with a couple of cases of ammunition. We scampered around like children in a candy store, trying to ignore the occasional skeletons we found mixed with some of the candy. The pandemic that swept Nevada a couple of years earlier had been thorough.

We loaded all the food and grain we could find in Austin, along with the best of what hardware we could scavenge, into the wagon.

After three weeks of collecting, we prepared to leave Austin with quite a wagon train. Abby drove Bertha, now pulling its own trailer, filled with everything we could stack on it. I followed, riding on the stallion and controlling the reins to the mares that pulled the wagon, also loaded to the gills. I even stacked on the top of it all the working parts of the windmill and a small mill for grinding grain. The donkeys trailed behind on a lead rope with full packs on their backs.

Our journey began as the sun rose over the mountains to the east. The first leg down the slope from Austin, a drop of three hundred feet in less than a mile, went pretty fast. I had read up on wagon brakes, so I knew to tie them down to keep the wagon from overrunning the horses. That first mile took us ten minutes.

I checked with our mapping software, and saw that at the bottom of the hill we began a long flat drive of twelve miles to the next small rise and another twelve after that to the mountain pass that followed. The temperature climbed as Abby drove ahead a measured mile on the old U.S. 50 roadbed and waited as I brought along the team and wagon. It took thirty minutes before I reached the rig. Dust covered the horses and me, and all of us needed water.

I had brought a ten-gallon can of water, and I soon realized that might not be enough. We each took a small swallow and let the horses drink a couple of quarts each. They wanted more.

"Abby, this is a problem. We are 110 miles from Fallon where we hope there will be some kind of water, but I don't think there is any water between here and there. It just took us half an hour to go the last mile. That's about two miles an hour. If we could average eleven hours each day, we are five days away from the next water, and I think the horses will drink all our water by tomorrow and would give out long before we reached Fallon. This ten gallons plus the forty we are carrying in the rig's tank is not going to last that long." I sat down in the shade of the rig and scratched my head.

"So what are we going to do?" she asked.

I thought a minute and made a decision. "We have to limit what we try to carry. We will leave the wagon and put packs on the horses. We pick out those things that can most help us survive, and leave the rest here alongside the road. Maybe someday we can come back and pick it up, but we cannot take all this with us."

"What about the horses?"

"They should be able to do about thirty or forty miles a day if they are not loaded down. That means we take three days to get to Fallon, and that should be doable."

"Can we carry enough water to get through?"

"I'm going to take the horses back to Austin and load up with more water. I saw some plastic bottles and bags in one of the old stores I can use. You can start sorting through the stuff in the rig and on the trailer and wagon." I kissed her on the cheek and unhitched the horses from the wagon. Turning the stallion around, I headed back up the slope to the town, leading the string of horses and donkeys on a tether. With my two pistols and rifle, I saw myself looking like a cowboy from out of the old west.

The surprise appeared to be mutual as I road Paint, my stallion, around a corner in the road and came face to face with three Angels on Hawgs, that is, three big dudes in black leathers and Hells Angels jackets on Harley Davidson motorcycles. They sat straddling their silent bikes in the center of the highway in the middle of Austin.

My rifle lay across the pommel of my saddle, my right hand around the trigger guard. I pulled on Paint's bridle and he reared, pawed the air, and settled back to the pavement. I moved him around to the right and my rifle pointed in the general direction of the three visitors.

"Howdy," I said in my most brusque voice. I reached up to my hat and pulled it down closer over my eyes. "You folks looking for somethin'?"

The three bikers leaned over their handlebars, watching me like they had never seen a cowboy, or a horse. The one on the right looked belligerent, but not enough to contest my right to be there with the rifle weaving around in front of him.

The middle rider reached up and pulled off the helmet that shielded her shiny red hair. It tumbled out and spread across her shoulders. "No, we're only looking for some fuel, and we certainly didn't expect to find anyone. But I guess you're a local. What we would really like is some regular gasoline or ethanol for these bikes. Do you know if there is any gasoline in this town?"

I liked her matter-of-fact attitude. I pushed my hat back up and responded in kind. "I found some diesel, but I didn't look to see if the other fuel tanks contained anything. You might check out the fueling station back up in the second block."

"Where do you live around here?" she asked.

"I don't live here," I replied. "My wife and I stopped here three weeks ago with a broken transmission, and we're getting ready to leave, heading west." I asked, "Where're you headed?"

I figured from her face the woman must be in her mid-thirties. She said, "We came out of the hell that is now Nebraska, hoping to find something safer out west, maybe in California. We made it this far, but we've almost run out of fuel. There just isn't much gasoline or ethanol anymore. Do you mind if we look around?"

I laughed. "Hell, I don't own this town, and we spent several weeks looking around ourselves and picking up things, so I don't see any reason you can't look as well."

"Where is everyone?"

I shook my head. "As near as I can tell, everyone in this town either left or died of some disease about two years ago, and there hasn't been anybody to come along to even bury them. You'll find some skeletons around. Don't mess with them, and they won't stink up the place too much. We haven't gotten sick from anything, so whatever the plague that killed them, it seems to be gone."

I still watched the two on either side of the lady doing the talking. They sat with their helmets on, and I could tell nothing about them. Finally, I asked, "What about your partners?"

She smiled. "It's okay, kids. Take off your helmets."

The two riders reached up to unbuckle their helmets and pull them up over their heads. Two more fire-engine red mops appeared, one above a girl that looked to be fourteen and the other on a boy the same age. "Let me introduce my twins, Jack and Jill. I'm Marsha Swanson, formerly Marsha Hardy out of Osceola, Iowa."

"I'll be damned," I exclaimed. "Your dad's name is Paul, isn't it?"

She looked at me in surprise and said, "Yes, how do you know?"

"My dad talked about my Uncle Paul who lived in Iowa. Told me of Paul's daughter named Marsha. I'm your cousin, Sam Hardy, from Sacramento. It looks like red hair runs in the family."

She smiled and said, "Well, I'll be damned. Hi, Cousin Sam."

"Hey, let me get my wife." I took out my two-way radio and called, "Abby, come on back up here. We're having a family reunion." I told her of the new faces, and she said she would bring Big Bertha back into town within thirty minutes.

Later that evening the five of us sat around a campfire built from fallen house timbers in the middle of the street, talking about our experiences and what the future might hold. When the subject of age came up, Marsha told me, "I'm thirty-four and my kids are fourteen."

Marsha married a farmer named Ted Swanson who worked with her father, Paul, on two thousand acres of corn in Iowa, just east of Osceola. The family did well selling the corn to the ethanol plants until the water wells went dry and the weather turned too hot. Two years in a row the corn did not make any grain, and then the grasshoppers arrived and ate up the next year's crop as it came out of the ground.

Ted died when his tractor rolled on him, and her father died of a heart attack soon after that. With the farm mortgaged to the hilt, the bank demanded payment on the farm loan and threatened to foreclose. Marsha just handed the bank officer the keys to the house, told them where to shove it, and she and the kids hopped on their bikes and headed west.

They carried everything they owned in their bike saddle-packs and wrapped in their tent rolls. Marsha wisely collected gold coins over the years as a hobby. She said, "I've got over two hundred ounces of gold stowed away in my bike packs. I'm not sure just how much it's worth, but at least we've got a grubstake."

I smiled. "At today's prices, you're over half a million dollars equivalent rich. Take my advice and keep it under cover. It may be worth more."

Marsha told me of the travels across the Midwest to reach Nevada. "The families back in the hills in Nebraska don't care much for anyone else. We traveled the back roads, and in the small towns most of the folks there didn't want us around. We found fuel and some food, but at times it got dicey."

Jill said, "We spent some time on the Interstate. It's pretty-well destroyed by the long-hauler trucks, but if we took our time we could avoid most of the big pot-holes and get out of the way of the other traffic. One time we went into one of the larger towns, and some of the locals chased after us. We outran the ogres before they could kill us and take our bikes."

"Things got better when we reached Wyoming, because we didn't meet as many people," Jack explained, "but I-80 was still a hard drive. People in towns along the freeway use coal and oil from the local mines and wells, but they don't grow much in the way of food. Their supply of food and such comes from the long-haul truckers."

Jill added, "When we got near Salt Lake, we could see that there would be even more trouble on I-80, so that's why we came south to travel old Highway 50."

Abby asked, "Did you kids go to school when you lived on the farm?"

Jill answered, "We went to public schools in Osceola up to the fourth grade, but Mom took us out after the fundamentalists took it over and started teaching religion instead of knowledge. That's when we started home education."

Jack added, "We helped with the chores and running the farm. Dad kept us pretty involved with the day-to-day operation. We both learned to drive the tractor and plow a straight line. But life got pretty hard."

Later that night, when the reception improved, we all listened to the short-wave radio. One commentator reported on troubles in southern California. "Our government has been taken over by the criminal cartels that came in from Mexico. Society is now broken, and anarchy is the common approach to meeting your neighbor." Another commentator reported on the riots along the coast in Santa Barbara and in Bakersfield. Very little fuel or electricity could be found, little food existed, and pollution contaminated most of the water sources.

I told Marsha and her kids how water became the southland's biggest problem. California started working on their Great Thirst initiative in 2028, building up the reservoirs and storing more water. They arranged to send all the King and Kern river water south, and the farmers on the west side of the valley screamed, but those in charge said people in the city needed water more than they needed food. That became more and more of a problem as sources of good water ran out and power to pump the water became more sporadic.

Our conversation around the fire turned to our own future. I said, "We must stick together as a family, and we can complete the journey from Austin across the dry lakes of Nevada to California with the horses and much of what we collected. It all depends on having a good plan for providing fuel and water for the trip. It's vital to reach the other side of the desert with the best of resources, and these horses are vital to our future. They will need to be nurtured if they are to make it with us." Everyone agreed.

We learned a lot on the trip from Austin to California. We knew it would be a long trek, and at times the winds across the dry lakes would make travel very difficult. Initially, we planned for a trip to Fallon, but after checking on conditions in Fallon, and then in Reno, we decided we needed to target Truckee at the foot of the Sierra Nevada Mountains as our destination to be safe.

We developed a way to make it. Using Austin's supply of both water and fuel, Marsha, Jack, and Jill made several trips on their bikes to hide caches alongside the route ahead of us. I rigged small trailers for them to pull with the supplies, so they could do an adequate job of it. They made several journeys ahead to lay the reserves so we would find the supplies we needed when we reached our camping spots along the way.

While preparing for the big move, I set up my Internet satellite system and began researching our final destination. Abby and I had already selected a campground called Lake of the Springs in the foothills above Marysville in California as our destination. It would be August by the time we reached Truckee, and we wanted to make it over the mountain passes before any storms started. I read the stories about the Donner party and did not want to repeat their experience. However, we also did not want to venture too far into the Sacramento Valley for fear of running into the hordes beginning to savage the southern parts of the valley.

By mid-June our convoy began its journey. Marsha and the kids headed out on their Harleys, loaded with fuel and water. Abby drove Big Bertha, pulling the trailer piled high with goods, and I road Paint, leading the horse and donkey team with a wagon loaded with water and straw. We averaged about twelve miles a day, from one cache to the next, taking it easy so as to not stress the livestock.

The shock Abby and I felt when we reached Reno overcame us. We remembered spending an evening in the car four years before while Theo and Hank went to gamble on the strip, but now the casinos stood silent and black. Downtown Reno had died.

We drove up the river to Truckee. Little water ran down the riverbed, and the pools looked stagnant. In Truckee we found a colony of people trying to live there even when sustainable farming was impossible. They told us of their worry about receiving enough food during the winter. Marsha traded one of her gold coins to fill the fuel tanks for the motor home and the bikes. They would have taken food instead if we had any to spare.

Occasional trains still ran along the rail lines over Donner summit, hauling food to the interior and resources back to California. Some long-haulers lined up to follow the Interstate over the summit. We joined them and headed up the grade to Donner. Frost and land slippage cracked the roadbed into massive blocks of rough concrete with interspersed gravel. I kept to the shoulder with the horses and wagon.

Once we reached the summit, we drove near a raging forest fire to get to old Highway 20. We headed over to the rim of the American River and then down to Nevada City. We encountered several groups along the way, most of them ready to fight to protect their holdings, but neither of us challenged the other.

Turning west on Highway 20, we continued down to Oregon Flat and then north to Lake of the Springs. On the last day of August we reached our new home, but disappointment almost drove us away. The outline of the lake nestled between the hills, but the reservoir stood less than half full of nearly stagnant water. We saw very few people in the area. Our struggles to return to northern California had ended, but a new set of worries awaited us.

The five of us found a camping place near the lake, and we settled in. Others in our new community drifted in, and they all seemed gaunt and depressed. We made their acquaintance, and they sat down to talk. The Lake people kept telling us of their troubles, not of their plans. They acted already lost and without hope.

Our arrival changed some of their feelings. Over the next few weeks we learned that the people who lived next to Lake of the Springs were not the only inhabitants of the area. There were several parasites that had preyed upon the Lake people as they called themselves, demanding food and other articles of value.

One incident told us much about the area and the people, and it also demonstrated to me the kind of support I had in my family.

Jack and Jill walked alongside the lake a week later with one of the Lake people who lived there, looking for a place that might serve as a good fishing spot. They had seen some activity in the water that suggested larger fish feeding near the surface, and they hoped to lure the fish to take their bait.

As they rounded a tree on the path beside the lake, a dirty old man dressed in rags stepped in front of them and held out his hand. "Give me some food; give me your bait," he said.

Jill, who was in the lead, drew back and looked at the man. "You've got to be kidding, and besides you stink. Get out of our way."

He brandished a stick and replied, "Give me some food or I'll beat you to a pulp."

"Jack, did you hear what that piece of trash said he would do to me? Do you think I should teach him a lesson?" she asked.

"Jill, just don't be too hard on him. I know he needs a bath, but it wouldn't do to contaminate the lake water any more than it already is. If you throw him uphill maybe he will start running in that direction and get the hell out of here."

Their woman companion from the Lake group cried, "You've got to feed him, else he will come and tear up our camp."

"Give me some food," the old man yelled.

Jill stepped forward and struck the man in the face with a karate chop using the side of her hand. "There, eat those teeth of yours, and get out of here before you make me really mad."

The vermin fell to the side of the trail, and then scrambled up and began to climb up the hill. A low whimper came from his broken lips.

The woman from the Lake group appeared astounded. "You ran him away. Now you've stirred up those around us who will steal our food." She turned and ran back toward her camp.

Jack said, "Jill, this does not look so good. We're living with a frightened bunch of losers."

This incident typified the kind of skirmish we fought to protect our camp. After a time the Lake people began to understand the need to protect what was theirs, but they were always reluctant to do so. For the most part they depended upon us to provide the protection.

At least it felt great to bring our family together. I knew that the five of us together as one had more of a chance to find a way to survive. Unfortunately, the land around the lake could not support the number of people who lived in the area, not even by farming the sides of the hills. Our family soon agreed we needed companions stronger than the Lake people to survive in this new land of California.

Puter said "End of file Chap-9."

"Class, we know little about Sam's cousins, but I am sure we will learn more. Knowing the Hardy family is larger is a great occasion and finding for our group."

CosandJo burst out, "And there are more making up our family. Sam and his cousins must make up our roots."

"CosandJo, quiet," the ProfSir said with a huff. "We still do not know if these are our ancestors."

Chapter 10: The River Tribes

January 21, 2040

The next morning the archeological group spread across the mounds of Alban looking for more remains of the past civilization. They found a few artifacts, but nothing to compare to SueJa's music box. That evening they gathered for the next reading from Sam Hardy's memoirs.

The ProfSir positioned himself on his pillows and spoke, "Today Sam tells us about how the founders of the Sutherlin tribe spent their first year in California at Lake of the Springs and then moved to be nearer the Feather and Sacramento rivers. But the starving hordes from the south began to plague their tribe, searching for something to eat."

CosandJo asked, "In history class we discussed the great wars that happened during this time. Is this how they began?"

"Yes, the population of the land divided into two parts: those who would try to sustain themselves and those who would try to live on the efforts of others. In the end, this division led to full-scale warfare."

"Puter, please say to us the next file, Chap-10," said ProfSir ElderJan.

Marsha, Abby, and I began to doubt that we had found a permanent home at Lake of the Springs soon after our arrival. The hilly land around the lake had few areas that could be farmed, and the thin soil would not grow lush crops. During the autumn of the year 2039, we often ran short of food. We were learning the first principle of how to live a sustainable existence: location, location, location.

Earlier Internet communications with the folks at the lake indicated it would be a good place for us to seek shelter, and they wanted our talents. The disappointment when we arrived hurt. The destitution and low morale of the people we found surprised us.

Most of Marysville and Yuba City had disappeared in the floods of 2036, and refugees from the Feather and Yuba river valleys stripped the surrounding land of its crops and animals. As supplies dwindled, a group of older residents from the flooded city retreated to the park in the hills, settled around the lake, and adopted a low profile.

The Lake people did little planning for how to localize their life and live off the land. Their memories remained focused on going to a store where they could purchase food, or, as later happened, accepting handouts from the government. At that time, what remained of the state government brought in a few staples for distribution in Marysville and other locations in the area every other week, as if by rote. There appeared to be no organized purpose in what the agencies did. The authorities made no plans on how to continue if and when their supplies ran out.

After we joined the group and explained a few problems with their planning, some residents endeavored to start gardens. Other members began making organized runs into the valley to find food. For the most part it was a matter of harvesting what grains they could find around the edges of the old rice and wheat fields. That grain could be used as food for the livestock or ground into a crude kind of flour. But most of them still relied on the government food-trucks that drove to the area from down around Sacramento once every other week.

One night in early November, after the Lake people had drifted off to their huts, my family sat around our fire pit sucking the marrow out of the bones of a wild turkey I had snared the day before. Our dog Hilda worried with the remains of a cottontail she and her surviving pup had chased down around dusk. We all moved closer to the blowing coals, bundled in our warmest coats and coverings, and I shoved a broken branch into the fire to create more heat. A cool nip in the air affirmed that the weather would turn much colder by morning.

Abby broached the subject we'd talked about more and more. "Sam, we've been here for a couple of months, but I already think we need to move on, to be part of a larger community."

My cousin Marsha, nine years my elder and her fifteen-year-old twins Jack and Jill nodded their heads in agreement.

"Yeah, it seems like all the folks here know how to do is to beg and tear things down," said Jack. "Old Man Jefferson asked if I would help him take shingles off the old clubhouse to use as firewood. Of course, if we did that then the roof would be certain to leak, and the building would be even more of a problem and of no use to any of us."

Marsha added, "We're just too vulnerable out here by ourselves. One of the roving gangs is going to come along and steal everything we have if we don't do more. This tribe doesn't have the gumption to fight for what's theirs. They should be sending out more guard parties to clear the area of the trash that's gathering around here—it can't always be us who do it."

I felt reluctant, but at the same time I knew Abby and the others were right. I had not told them of my encounter on my turkey hunt with another vagrant working his way through our area. I noticed him because of his smell, and I always carried a pistol and a rifle. He cut and ran when I threatened him. I was not afraid to show force. But someday, someone would bushwhack me, and then Abby and Marsha would have no one to warn and protect them. I declared, "You guys are right. It's time to do something."

Abby continued, "Our skills are not suited for our family to be farmers. Sam, admit it, neither you nor I can get anything to grow, though Marsha and the kids can. We are better suited to help the farmers. We need to band together with people who understand which end of the plant goes into the ground and who are more motivated than the losers here."

Jill suggested, "And let's find a group who understands both horses and bikes." She had traded her Harley for a horse, but still enjoyed sitting on Jack's bike. Of course, without gasoline or ethanol, Jack's Harley had just sat in place for the past two months.

I pointed out to my family, "We have the horses, so we have something to offer any group. And my experience in fuels should be a factor. Abby, you're a good teacher, and you know all those languages. Marsha and the twins know their way around a farm. We should be kind of picky about who we team up with. My supply of ammo is getting low, but we still have some firepower. Not only that, but I've been working on building long-bows for each of us."

Jill chimed in, "Hey, Jack and I learned some things at the martial arts school back in Iowa, so we don't have to shoot anybody."

I laughed, "I know. You proved it with that vagrant when we first arrived."

"You mess with one Swanson, and you mess with all the Swansons west of the Rockies." She looked around at the incredulous grins. "Well, at least the strongest ones."

I laughed again and said, "Thanks for reminding me, and I hope you look out for us Hardys. Someday when I want someone to command my troops, I'll call on you and your brother." Little did I know that time was not far away. "In any case, I agree. We need to find something better."

Abby smiled. "I knew you would agree. So I did some checking."

I rolled my eyes. It always happened that way.

She told us about her surfing on the Internet to ask around about young tribes that seemed to be forming. "Your diploma as a Ph. D. in chemical engineering is a meal ticket, and it allows us to pick the tribe we want. Only an experienced organic farmer is considered a better recruit."

Abby showed us her short list of three possibilities, all in Northern California or Oregon. We talked into the night, putting together our inventory of skills and possessions that would contribute to a sustainable society.

During November the weather remained cool, and in December the surface of the lake froze. Talking and planning what to do came easy, but the life of the status quo became an easy trap, and we put off taking action on moving. Instead, we spent more and more of our time helping the original group at Lake of the Springs.

During the rains of January, three elders from Lake of the Springs drove their wagon to Marysville for the next quota of rations from the state. But the food did not arrive, and the people who had gathered to receive their sustenance turned ugly. Fighting broke out between the supplicants and the providers. The authorities called in a gang of thugs to clear the area around the distribution center. One of our elders died from a blow to his head in the riot, and the thugs wrecked our wagon. The two remaining representatives rode the horses back to the Lake and reported what had happened.

Everyone in the group except our family decided they could do nothing. They would have to try again next week to obtain their quota of food. The Hardys and Swansons began to pack for travel.

In February 2040, I read on the Internet about a new enclave in the Oroville area on the banks of the Feather River, not more than thirty miles from us. They descended from one of the urban gangs down in Oakland and still followed some of the old protocols like facial tattoos for identification. But they had learned a lot of technology and had become very practical about how and where they lived. Their website told about what and how they did things. They did not do synthetic drugs. They would use plant opiates, but nothing manufactured. They called themselves the New Krips.

I contacted the group by email and sent them resumes of my family and a list of what resources we could offer. After a week an email response came back telling us to come on in, and they provided a password to use for safe conduct. I remember they said to tell everyone we were Tinkerbells.

That evening around the community campfire, I explained that the five of us were leaving the Lake of the Springs group, and several of the original members wept. I explained why we thought we had to move, and invited any of them to go with us, but they all declined. Old Man Jefferson said, "This is our place. This is where we gathered to be safe. We will be fine. If you must go, God speed."

Two days later we loaded our belongings on our horses and in our wagon and left our little lake in the foothills. I removed the solar and power systems but left the shell of the old motor home for the people at Lake of the Springs to use for whatever they wanted.

It took three days and two trips for the Tinkerbells to move to Oroville. The New Krips had a small supply of ethanol, and the Swansons insisted on bringing their remaining motorcycle along.

The flatter land next to the Feather River meant people could maintain small farm plots. Water flowed in the river, and a group of people in the tribe grew grains, beans, and some vegetables. The tribe had a herd of work animals. Only when one of the animals aged or otherwise became unproductive did the gang butcher the animal and eat meat.

Horses were important in our new society. Our two mares were in foal, and soon we began trading stud services of our little stallion and the donkey jack for more mares. Our horse and mule herd grew.

The horses attracted the attention of vagrants roaming the area, and several times we fought off bandits who seemed to think the horses were for the taking. We lost a mare, but we compensated by hanging the next horse-thief we caught. Apparently, word got around and the horse thieves stayed away from the New Krips.

Best of all, the hydroelectric generators in the Feather River dam produced electrical power—at least a small amount of it. There were several experts in the New Krips tribe who knew how to control and even repair the turbines and generators, so the system remained viable. We used the electricity within the tribal grounds and arranged to sell some power to those on the outside.

In 2043 an economy of sorts still existed. Many people used U.S. dollar bills to exchange for goods and services, but you could often get a better deal by bartering. You just had to have something to trade.

I asked the head of the New Krips why they called it a gang, and the leader explained it was because they governed the group like a gang. They elected a single leader, and everyone obeyed. Everyone must swear allegiance to the gang. And everyone had to wear an identifying tattoo. People who violated their oath were executed without remorse.

My family all received our identifying tattoos on the side of our foreheads and went through the induction ceremonies at the foot of the dam. As I turned twenty-eight, I realized we had spent two years back in California, and things were peaceful. We all made friends among our fellow gang members. Abby started teaching the youngsters that were in the area, and I did lots of work on the Internet for the gang. Several times I gave instructions on how to use the Internet.

One day one of the boys reported seeing a very large fish in the river. Most people did not believe his story, but a few of us went to the river to see for ourselves. To our amazement, we saw several large fish breaking the top of the water in the pool below the dam. I recognized them as salmon. The salmon run on the Feather River had finally been re-established.

We caught a few of the fish and ate everything. Later we learned how to dry the fish for later consumption. Our general health improved after that.

In January 2045, business within the state of California collapsed. A better way of putting it is that the economy as we had known it collapsed. People stopped accepting U.S. currency. They demanded goods or some kind of commodity. Even physical gold became suspect.

With my background in economics, I found it interesting to see how everyone's attitudes changed almost overnight. They just no longer trusted pieces of paper that someone declared to be worth something. The rapid change in attitude surprised me.

I believe one of the reasons for the collapse of money turned out to be that the supply of liquid fuel dropped to near zero. The New Krips, and then everyone else in the area, ran out of fuel. You could not find any gasoline, ethanol, diesel, or propane. Truck tankers and railcars no longer came from the Bay Area with any petrochemicals.

Without fuel, food became more and more scarce, and most everyone had no reserve. People began to scavenge for whatever they could find.

The New Krips had stored some grains and beans away, and soon they established a 24/7 guard around their fortified granary.

Pressure mounted from the scavengers and soon there were fights for livestock and food, and the thieves collected whatever they could. After some discussion, the New Krips established a vigilante committee for the area around Oroville. They maintained guards throughout the encampment. The first time they caught someone stealing, he or she received a warning and a tattoo in the middle of their forehead marking them as a thief. The committee then took them to the side of the Feather River downstream from our encampment and threw them in. A few were unable to make it back to land downstream, but many did.

If they caught someone with a thief tattoo already in place, the vigilantes tied a concrete block to their leg before they threw the thief into the river. Soon the law and order crowd had control. As people starved or drowned, the problem disappeared.

Marsha and her twins became active in the security section of the New Krips, and worked hard to keep the vagrants away from our territory. Jill astounded me one day when she came home from leading a patrol into the nearby hills with a bloody scalp lock tied to her belt. "I didn't kill him. I just hit him on the side of the head. I couldn't give him a tattoo right there, so I took his hair. When he woke up, I prodded his butt with my knife to move him along. I don't think he or his friends are going to come back."

We heard about the immense destruction in and near the larger cities to the south that occurred with riots and battles between different urban mobs. The strongest people spread like locusts out from the urban areas across the land in search of food. Chaos reigned supreme. Everyone looked for food, anything to stay alive. But most just stayed in the cities and towns, waiting for someone to help them, waiting to die.

We used the Internet to contact the people we still knew in Sacramento and Davis and pleaded with them to come north to Oroville, but most decided to stay where they were. After a series of riots swept through central California, we could no longer contact them. We feared they had been lost in the anarchy that enveloped the densely populated areas.

Word came on the Internet that several more nuclear plants had come online in southern California, but we never saw any evidence of additional power up in the Oroville area. The national grid had been cut apart by then. We had hydroelectric power from the Oroville dam, but it only serviced the local area. In time, even that service deteriorated, as the people who knew how to run the turbines and generators were lost.

In 2045 I turned thirty at Oroville. I felt ancient at the time because so much had happened to change the world. I took a position of management and responsibility for the gang. Abby worked as my assistant.

I simplified the gang rules to be very clear. People who were not a member of the gang would receive absolutely nothing. There would be no mercy, not even a quick killing, unless they attacked a gang member or some of our property. We stored all food and other supplies behind the walls of our fort, determined to defend it to the death.

Life proved hard for the New Krips, and we fought for everything we had. We protected our fields and animals. We defended our water. We coddled our power generation equipment: solar, wind, and some hydroelectric. During that year the supply of petrochemicals disappeared, and the last engine died for lack of lubricating oil.

We did have some hydrogen generation capabilities based on solar electrolyzing water into H_2 and O_2. This allowed us to operate some of the fuel cells we had collected, as well as some of the H_2 transports. But for the most part, we relied on horses.

The weather grew more and more wild. The hot winds continued to blow through the valley, and once in a while a violent storm blew down from the mountains. The danger of a range fire during electrical storms was extreme, especially among some of the old dead timber stands. One of the reasons for staying close to the river bank was to have at least one side protected from the fires.

California drifted further and further into chaos.

At one time in the spring of 2046, I told my family things could not get any worse up and down California. Lawlessness reigned supreme, and insanity ruled most of the population outside our group. Strong gangs such as the New Krips were able to hold an area and fight off the attacks from the frenzied mobs. As it turned out, I missed the mark by five years: things became a lot worse around 2050.

I found a news report on the Internet that a nuclear war had started in the Middle East. It appeared that the Iranians attacked Israel first, and then the Israelis retaliated. Before long everyone with atomic bombs dropped them on everybody else. All the big oil fields became targets and were destroyed, or at least put out of operation for the foreseeable future. It occurred to me that this should slow down the CO_2 emissions.

Then atomic bombs began to fall in Pakistan and India, and then China. It took two years for the final tally to be estimated, and the estimated toll proved awesome. Casualties directly from the bombs totaled only twenty-five million, but the estimates for the starvation and pestilence that followed were for more than five billion. What with the starvation of the previous thirty years, the population of the earth dropped to below one billion in less than half a century, an 85 percent reduction.

ElderJan stopped the Puter and said, "Over half the population of the world was in Asia and Southeast Asia. So much of the world's population died in so few years."

CosandJo asked, "Do we know if any survived?"

The ProfSir answered, "We recently heard some radio traffic that seems to come from that part of the world. The language is similar to some Chinese dialects. But we really do not know the state of that part of the world. I expect the university will send a scouting probe in that direction in the next few years."

"Puter, please continue with Chap-10," said ProfSir ElderJan.

North America had its problems with weather, droughts, and monster hurricanes along the coast of the Gulf of Mexico and on the Pacific coast. Food did not exist in any of the major cities, and people wandered around searching for sustenance. Farmlands were scavenged for whatever people could find. The few farmer-types who tried to establish crops often lost their plants before they were even halfway grown.

The New Krips gang grew in size and diversity as a few migrants joined the group. Some became religious fundamentalists, and they tried to impose their moral judgments on everyone. Others adopted fascism as their approach and demonstrated their willingness to control whoever they could. A few became isolationists, trying to figure out how to survive alone. Internal conflicts approached the point where the New Krips needed to split apart and form new tribes.

In March 2046 Abby and I and my cousins moved with a like-minded group of survivalists from Oroville over to the Sacramento River near Red Bluff. There we founded a commune and called ourselves the Jakes of the Sacramento River. Our governmental approach was more tribal than gang-based.

We accepted people into our group who believed much as we did and would accept us. Everyone appreciated my chemical engineering and electronics expertise and Abby's language and teaching abilities. They also liked my horses, solar systems, and satellite communications equipment.

The Sacramento River Jakes group made extensive use of solar power, and we built a thermal-solar farm near our commune. We had some innovative technology that allowed us to build more efficient collectors for a varied terrain. We used small steam engines to drive generators to produce power to irrigate fields and hothouses where we could grow a variety of food.

The salmon run grew stronger in the Sacramento River each year. My family settled in and quickly became an integral part of the Jakes Tribe.

We heard a report that the sea level continued to rise at a prodigious rate, reaching over a meter higher than at the start of the century. On the coast, most of the port facilities and docks had been lost, along with many of the refineries situated next to the water. Ocean shipping became pretty much a thing of the past. The economy shifted to depending upon locally grown food. That would work okay in California near the rivers, but there was a definite limit to what could be grown.

Abby and I enjoyed our time with the Jakes. During the next four years, there were some sporadic raids by the roving hordes, but the Jakes were strong and well organized. We defended our territory well and kept our losses to a minimum.

The whole world seemed to be drifting back to an agrarian society. Civilization had little room for a hunter-gatherer, because the land had nothing to hunt and you had to plant everything you wanted to gather. If you did not have the means to grow your food, you went hungry. And to get water you had to live near a large supply, like a major river.

The weather stayed dry, and the smaller streams dried up during the summer and fall. Only the big rivers had a continuing flow, and even they stopped when the water stopped pouring through the outlets of the dams.

Shasta Lake dam proved to be a case in point. For a while the power turbines in the great dam ran every day to provide electricity to the surrounding area, but after a time they fell into disrepair and stopped running. Those attending the dam just shut the gates, and for a while no water ran down the Sacramento.

A group of us went to the dam to find out why no water flowed. Everyone in charge had left the area, and what we found was that the reservoir behind the dam must completely fill before water could run over the floodgates and down the river. That meant that if a major rain storm struck northern California and filled the reservoir, the river could suddenly and catastrophically flood.

After examining the dam, we determined there to be an exhaust spillway in the base of the dam that could be opened partway to permit a continuous flow of water down the river. We opened the exhaust to what we believed to be the average flow and left it that way.

Our estimate proved to be pretty good, and the Sacramento River ran at a constant rate for several years. The level of the lake behind would rise to near the top of the floodgate during the winter and then drain during the summer and fall. This worked until the winter of 2049 when the lake filled entirely in the first early rain and then flooded the valley below for the next two months as the rains continued.

In 2048 we had heard a report that all of the Arctic ice cap had melted during the winter, and Greenland lost all its ice. All of it. Someone reported that the earth had been reduced to 20 percent of its carrying capacity at the beginning of the century, what with the Middle East oil gone.

When the Sacramento River flooded in the winter and early spring of 2049, it marked the end of what little organized civilization we were beginning to develop in the central California valley. Society simply broke down.

We could still communicate with satellite Internet and find a few channels of satellite TV run by the government. They kept offering advice and giving us some news. We produced most of our food ourselves by local farming, though there were still occasional food shipments coming up the I-5 interstate road from the government in Sacramento.

Then those food shipments failed. They simply quit coming. We heard that it was a combination of lack of supplies coming in by boat and increasing unrest in the urban areas. On top of that, much of the farming disappeared under water when the Sacramento River overflowed its banks and inundated the small farms that had sprung up.

It took a while for the situation to sink in for the refugees in the camps scattered throughout central California. They would get no more food.

Stealing became even more rampant, and then riots broke out as different groups tried to find something to eat. The refugees picked the land clean, and the Jakes gang adopted a bunker mentality to protect our fields. Our fields were not ready for harvest, but the mobs would have overrun them and destroyed the crops trying to find something if we allowed it. We suddenly had a war on our hands, and we had to treat it as a war.

Every member of the Jakes rode or walked the perimeter as an armed guard at least ten hours a week. When we detected a prowler, a call went out for reinforcements, and we would bring in a large and powerful strike force. Our orders said to kill all who attacked: take no prisoners, leave no survivors.

I remember in the fall of 2049 when things finally settled down around Redding. A group of us expanded into a collective on Cottonwood Creek and did sustenance farming to produce food.

I had been elected the leader for the collective. There were about thirty-five people in my group.

Deaths continued around us. We became even more possessive about what we had and would let people join us only when they offered something of value to us. We maintained contact with other enclaves and started to trade with them, mostly in people of talent.

Over time our collective grew to ninety, and we farmed almost forty-five acres. We irrigated with water from the Sacramento River. The old reservoir above us stayed full most of the time, and many people camped around its shores.

Then the winds started blowing away our topsoil.

We heard over satellite how the plains states returned to desert conditions. The Dakotas, Nebraska, Kansas, Oklahoma, and West Texas looked like the Dust Bowl of one hundred twenty years before.

The population in the eastern states of the old U.S. dropped precipitously from starvation and disease. Only the southern states managed to provide enough local food to sustain their populations. Things did not get better, they got worse.

By the middle of the century, the weather patterns of Baja California reached north into the Central Valley. Drought conditions prevailed, and the irrigation system could not keep up. With the drought came fires as the brush and trees on the slopes dried and died. When a fire started, no state fire crews came to fight it. Fires burned until they ran out of fuel.

Reports from Oregon and Washington told of increasing drought, but they still did reasonably well. When the weather turned stormy, the rains provided them with lots of water compared to what we received, at least in some locations. Their growing season had lengthened so they could get along.

Shortly after the first of the year 2050, Abby and I walked the west perimeter one night in the light of a full moon. We were suddenly attacked by a group of at least ten men and women. The first indication of something wrong sounded when I heard the slap of a bullet hitting Abby in the shoulder. She fell to the ground in a heap.

At the sound of the shot I dropped to the ground, ten feet away from Abby. She rolled over and began to fire from a prone position at the shadows that moved beyond the perimeter berm.

I grabbed my radio and broadcast. "Attackers at Westside marker three. We're receiving small arms fire. Man down. Ten attackers plus. Send response." I pushed my rifle in front of me and fired just behind the point where I had seen the flash of a gunshot in the dark. I heard the satisfying sound of someone taking my round in the chest, sort of a thud-whoof.

"Sam, watch behind you," Abby yelled.

I turned to see in the moonlight a large figure leaping at me from the side. I whipped my rifle around and fired a shot just as the hurtling body reached me, blasting a hole through his or her chest. The corpse fell on my rifle, and I had to bring my foot around to push it off my weapon.

I heard a scream, and turned to see another attacker striking Abby with a knife. I leapt from my crouch and slammed the butt of my rifle into the head of the attacker, knocking the ghoul aside. I fired shot after shot into the body of the attacker, and finally at those who I could see fleeing the scene.

Looking down, I saw that I was too late. Abby's head had almost been severed, and blood pulsed from her throat. I pulled my radio out and screamed "Medic, Medic!" Then I laid my other hand over her throat, trying to stop the flow of blood. Nothing helped. Abby died there in the sand alongside the Sacramento River.

I could not help it. I cried. Abby had been my soul mate for eighteen years, and we had done so much together. I felt empty.

"End of file Chap-10," the Puter said.

The group sat silent, stunned at how Sam's wife Abby had been lost.

"Was there some way to stop this kind of thing from happening?" asked SueJu.

CosandJo spoke first, "When you are dealing with savages, you have to treat them as savages."

ProfSir ElderJan said, "But, remember, these so-called savages were starving. You must protect yourself from someone who is starving. They have nothing to lose."

MeJe looked stricken and cried, "But Abby never had her baby."

ProfSir looked sad and replied, "No, and it was that kind of thing that Sam had been concerned about. It was not a time to raise a family."

"Then there must be someone else," exclaimed CosandJo. "Someone else must be our roots." There was silence in the tent.

Chapter 11: Retreat to Shasta

March 15, 2050

Leaving Albin, the troop continued for another sixty klicks along the west side of the Wilimet River to the mounds of Salem. The tent was pitched beside the river. Larger mounds could be seen on the opposite side of the water, but there was no bridge across the river to reach that area. The students spread out to search the smaller mounds in the immediate area.

When they gathered in the tent after their evening meal, ProfSir Elder-Jan asked, "Did anyone find an artifact of significance?"

CosandJo spoke first. "I found a statue on a pedestal. It must have been made from bronze. There was some corrosion, but it showed a good likeness to a man on a horse. I drew a picture of the statue and copied the inscription down for translation back at the university." He showed his drawing to the rest of the class.

"Good, such information will help us work out the history of this area."

MeJe said, "The area where I looked appeared to be from old buildings with concrete and cinder bricks. I did not find anything to collect."

ElderJan said, "That is about all I expected here. Someday we can return and search the other side. That is obviously where the large part of the city was.

"But in the meantime, we can continue to hear Sam Hardy's story. Today we hear how the River Tribes fought the Sacramento River War and then left the Sacramento Valley and moved to the north, hoping to escape the hordes from the south."

CosandJo asked, "There is a legend of that war in some of the old history sayings. Could it be as bad as the sayings give as truth?"

"We will find out about that war in the next file. Puter, please say to us file Chap-11," said ProfSir ElderJan.

In March 2050 I demanded the position of Tribal War Chief of the Sacramento River Jakes.

Abby, my wife of eighteen years, had been killed in a food fight in January. I did not take long to grieve. I thought long and hard about a way to work off my anger. Annihilation of the hordes of savages from the south became my soul-healing goal.

I knew the hordes tried to find anything they could in the way of food, but that could not excuse them for Abby's death. California started with thirty million more people than it could support, and for any to survive, those numbers had to be reduced to a sustainable level, somewhere much less than a million.

The day I turned thirty-five, the tribe voted and agreed I should lead them into war. I stood before them with my flaming red hair and beard and called for those young men and women who wished to survive to join my army. I called upon their emotions to exact from the invaders a thousand times the drops of blood they had taken from our kin. I told them we had no choice if any good part of humankind was to survive through our times. We had to destroy the hordes—every man, woman, and child—or at least drive them from our lands. I yelled over the applause, "I am your General. I will lead you to victory."

Some accused me of preaching ethnic cleansing and genocide, and I understood how they felt, but my rational conclusion was that opposing the parasites of a sustainable society was not only necessary, it was required. Otherwise, all of humanity would perish. I could offer no alternatives that allowed mankind to survive.

I appointed Jack and Jill Swanson as my military commanders, and we set out to become an army. I interviewed all the young people who wanted to join us, and with Jack and Jill's review, we placed the new volunteers into squads of responsibility: weapons, transport, provisions, recruitment, and security.

The weapons squad began to instruct and direct older members of the tribe on building a supply of metal-tipped lances and arrows. Salvage became the source for the metal and willows provided the shafts. A portion of the weapons supply group began to make machetes.

The transport squad collected horses, mules, and wagons. The intense breeding program I had begun five years ago paid off with a large herd of riding and pulling stock, though many of the animals had to be broken to a rider with the packsaddle on their back, or to the harness in front of a wagon or chariot. Since I had collected the jack and jenny in Nevada years before, we had a few mules, and they proved to be the calmest and strongest of the equine stock.

The provisions squad collected containers for carrying grain and water. We expected to live off the land most of the time, but needed a reserve supply for when we could not find local food and water.

The vital work of the recruitment squad included the responsibility of visiting our neighboring tribes up and down the Sacramento and Feather

Rivers and convincing them to join the Jakes in the coming war against the hordes. I worked many days with this squad in their visits.

Finally, the security squad took charge of training and ensuring the safety of our tribe. Jill commanded this group, and they practiced on those vagrants who encroached within three days of our tribal lands. Other recruits cycled through security as a matter of training for when we would go on the offensive.

The Jakes did not fight alone. At least fifty other gang-related farming enclaves much like ours lay scattered throughout the upper Sacramento Valley. Jack and I visited them all and told them of our goals. We made compacts with the other tribes along the river and planned how to cooperate against the hordes of migrants that kept invading our land to steal our food and livestock and kill members of our tribe.

I preached survival as our common goal. That meant we had no choice but to destroy the invaders. There could be no mercy. We would fight individual battles and coordinated campaigns. We all agreed our battles would be waged to the end.

Over the next year, as we organized for the coming war, the tribes fought multiple skirmishes along the Sacramento River to protect our land. Some of the enclaves fell, but most, like the Jakes, survived. With the tribes organized and on the offensive, the southern hordes began to starve. We would not feed them, and they knew nothing of how to farm for themselves. After a time many grew too weak to attack and offered to surrender, but we turned a deaf ear, as agreed. Otherwise, we would simply join those who were starving.

"Puter, pause here," said the ProfSir. "Class, this is one of the most distressing accounts I have heard about the conditions of the Great Collapse and the logic for what happened. We have identified Sam as a

Neu-human because he had a tail like us. Yet, one of our most vital traits is rational thinking. Yes, we feel emotion, but our decisions are made on pure logic, not the biases from the past history of the human race.

"Therefore, I must conclude that Sam spoke and operated from a logical conclusion that for the human race to survive there could only be a small portion of the population that could be part of that survival. Only those who were willing to live in a sustainable fashion and fend for themselves had a chance."

SueJa asked, "But is that moral? Isn't it everyone's right to survive?"

ProfSir ElderJan rubbed his brow and after a moment said, "No, survival is not a right guaranteed by nature. Nature is amoral. It operates with a rule called the survival of the fittest, and those who are not in a position by time or place or inclination or instinct to survive will not survive. Even today our tribe must practice control over our lives and reproductive tendencies to be sure that the fittest survive. For a species to survive, it cannot live by a rule where most survive at the expense of the total population.

SueJa said, "But it seems so cruel."

"Yes, it is, but such amorality is necessary. We should discuss these matters later this year in our classes back at the university. Puter, please continue."

In the spring of 2051, I gathered the collected Sacramento tribes together into a mounted army of eight hundred under my command. We marched south from near Redding through the valley, toward an agreed destination on the shores of the Sacramento Sea. I sent Jack with two hundred warriors along the foothills of the Sierras, while Jill with her two hundred screaming women scoured the west side of the valley. I lead the main troop of four hundred down the valley center along the course of the Sacramento River.

I established as our first objective the task of searching out any group who did not engage in productive work, and we simply eliminated them on the spot. There was not time for them to find some productive unit to join; they should have done this before we arrived.

Those residents with farms and implements were encouraged to join us in our cleansing of the land. Many joined our band, but a few refused. We noted those who declined for later attention and review, and we told them of our expectations for them to adopt sustainable living and join our group.

As we drove to the south, our army grew to over two thousand warriors, half mounted on horses, half marching behind the wagons. The wagons followed us as we crisscrossed the valley, searching for vagrants and collecting food to support our army. Using our machetes and bows, we routed any parasites who lived upon the works of others and gave them a short day to head south with their families. Those who did not heed our warning died. It proved to be an awful experience, but we believed that to be our only option to protect ourselves from those with no idea of how to live sustainably other than to steal food.

Jack, Jill, and I discussed the breakdown of civilization. By the end of 2051, we agreed that everyone, including ourselves, qualified as a savage, but that such an attitude had become necessary to survive. The cleansing of our lands continued, but the number opposing us diminished and lost all cohesion.

Sadly during the winter, Jack's squad ran into heavy resistance along the American River, and in an epic battle, he and twenty-five of his troops died in a surprise raid by the invaders. I would miss my cousin.

The next year in May, the collective army of the Sacramento Tribes ended their fighting and met in a great gathering on the banks of the Sacramento

Sea. Our Provisions squads caught fish from the Sacramento Sea and scoured the land around us for greens for a great celebration feast.

I spoke to the army of three thousand warriors gathered on the shores of the Sea. "You are the Survivors," I said. "You cleansed our land of the parasites who never learned the art of survival. You repelled the invaders from the south who only wished to steal our food and our stock and our women. You protected our tribal lands from the invading hordes. You are the good part of the human race.

"We no longer need to drive the invaders out—they are gone. They died in battle or starved." I paused and looked over my army. "We do not need all this land we cleansed, for there are some here who learned how to sustain themselves, how to grow food, how to be good neighbors. We will leave this land to them, and they will either learn to defend it themselves and keep the hordes from our tribes, or they will be overrun or killed by the hordes.

"Now is the time for us to return to our tribal homes. But all who remain here should remember that if the hordes return, we will come back and wipe them once again from this land."

By that fall the world returned to normal, at least as normal as we could make it.

I remember chatting later that year on the Internet with some who thought the current year was the most significant. In 2006 someone predicted the human population would peak at 8.9 billion in 2054 and begin to drop off at a slow pace. The best estimate I could find on the Internet said that as of 2054 the earth's population stood at 2.9 billion. The peak of 7.2 billion happened back in 2017 before the pandemics started. Droughts and lack of energy led to starvation, and the pandemics wiped out the weak to make up the difference.

At mid-century the population in the North American Federation stood at about two hundred million, with half of those in the contiguous United

States area. Mexico settled in at fifty million, and now eighty million lived in Alaska and Canada, most of whom migrated from the southern regions in recent years.

More and more the population divided into two groups. There were those who remained in the cities and suburbs, and those who had left the urban areas early in the emergency. As food production and supply for the cities became more difficult, the force of starvation drove the urban enclaves out to roam the adjoining lands in search of food and water. They became the hordes that infested all of California. Eventually, the majority of the city dwellers left their homes to become savages, the ones we fought in the Sacramento River Wars.

The original prediction for mean sea level had been twenty-five centimeters above 1900 levels by the middle of the century, but instead it rose 1.5 meters as the western Antarctic ice shelf continued to break up and fall into the sea. Estimates made mid-century predicted a rise of half a meter every ten years.

The transport system fast approached total disarray. Biodiesel fueled the trucks in the 2050s, but supply continued to diminish. Some cars still ran on hydrogen. Horses became an important commodity and found use for personal transport wherever possible. In 2054 most people who had no horses rode bicycles or walked.

The primary occupation of the land became that of farmer. Each family tribe had taken on the responsibility for farming from two to six acres, with most cultivation done by hand. Over the previous ten years a major effort had developed a supply of seeds for grains and vegetables. A number of orchards had been planted, and though irrigation systems were installed to pump water from the river to the fields, most was pumped through manual labor.

Salvage became a major industry as the locals stripped all former buildings and businesses of their useful parts for their collective use. The tribes established warehouses for various kinds of parts, like computers and other electronics, motor assemblies, solar, lighting, cooking, and so on.

Without precision metal working, the production of firearms ceased. We collected all available weapons. A few people knew how to create gunpowder so long as they could find the raw materials, though those chemicals became more and more scarce. People reloaded their own shells for lack of any other supplier.

The weapons of choice became the knife, machete, and pole. Some of the more advanced adopted the longbow and steel-tipped arrow.

You rarely saw powered vehicles. A few E-cars still existed, and some people traveled about in their H-cars. The primary source of electricity came from solar systems that had been installed in the previous twenty years. Excess solar capacity created hydrogen for the H-cars or for some of the stationary fuel cells.

The last commercial computer came off the production line in 2032. By 2050 new computers had become rare. In fact, almost no production of the electronic components used in computers or power production remained. As a result, the ongoing electronics salvage operations became the primary source of computing equipment, and a large cadre of people learned how to repair computers.

We used computers for two primary purposes in 2054. They processed emails, though smaller personal digital assistants also did this, and they provided Internet connections to the worldwide knowledge base.

Amazingly, with some of the larger server farms still existing, some financial transactions could still be processed over the Internet. A couple of my accounts from years past still contained resources, and I made arrangements to convert all such assets into useful items and somehow got them delivered to me. There were some amazing bargains on the online auction sites.

However, the quality of the Internet connection and service dropped at an alarming rate. Obviously, major segments of the net died over time. By 2052 I concluded that I should not expect the Internet connectivity to last much longer.

I also noticed deterioration in my satellite TV service. Fewer programs remained available, and the signals began to be sporadic. I checked with the providers and learned that their inability to replace the aging satellites in geosynchronous orbit accounted for most of the degradation. More and more of the satellites ran out of fuel for maintaining their position, and in future times they would all go off the air. I became much more interested in the reemergence of shortwave radio as a communication medium.

During the 2050s the declining availability of medicines proved to be the more significant loss. The large pharmaceutical companies stopped making their pills. The government could no longer pay, and medical insurance slipped into the past. Many of the specialty medications simply disappeared, and apparently all of the development of new medicines had ended by the middle of the century.

A few companies still made some of the basic remedies, and homebrew recipes for common medicines like aspirin and ibuprofen appeared on the Internet. But the more potent medicines for heart and cancer patients just disappeared once the black market dried up. For a while the death rate among the elderly soared, and the average age dropped.

The government attempted to maintain production facilities for the various flu vaccines, but even that effort shut down for lack of expertise to run it.

In 2055, as more and more technologies failed, we heard how the cities began falling apart big time. Many of the larger urban areas still held groups of sustenance stalwarts who strived to keep their cities alive by adopting new methods for food production and transportation. Unfortunately, their supplies of the basic infrastructure began to decay beyond the point of repair. Electric service became intermittent. Water became limited. And sewage disposal became an issue. Some food could be produced by local plots, but in most cases more needed to be shipped in, and those supplies disappeared sooner than expected.

The 2050s proved to be a time of significant shifting in the course of civilization. So many facilities on which the urbanites depended just disappeared. Without the complete set of technological tools, most of the mainstays could not survive. Within ten years our technology dropped back below the 1910 level.

In 2055 our group along the Sacramento River above Cottonwood Creek decided we should move. The climate continued to warm and become dryer and dryer. The Sacramento River even quit flowing for three weeks in 2054, and our efforts to irrigate our crops could soon become fruitless.

Even after our cleansing wars of 2051, we experienced an increasing number of raids from the remains of the cities, and we knew we needed to find a better place for defense.

Early in the year we sent a group over to the Pacific coast to check south for a good location. They found the valleys already occupied and involved with the traditions of grapes and wine. The locals did not want more people, only someone who would trade for their products.

The coast itself showed signs of being ravaged by large storms, and the roads in that area became almost impassable.

Another group set out to search north in the valley, and after three months they returned. They found a spot along the Sacramento River above the remains of Dunsmuir. It offered a good supply of water and farmland. A small enclave lived there in a town called Weed, and our group talked with them about joining. We would provide them with a stronger force for protection. They agreed that we should come.

The Jakes headed for Northern California as a survival enclave. We carried weapons for defense and seeds for planting.

We reached the town of Weed and set up camp. Our choice proved to be our best one yet, and we found the new people to be good additions. Our tribes merged into one.

I remember in 2058 when we received a report that a group in France succeeded in starting a fusion reaction and found the source for unlimited energy that would not add to global warming. We cried when we heard the news. Maybe somebody's great-great-grandchildren would someday benefit from that event, but we had to live with what we had.

Our tribe prospered, even as technology continued to fail. The weather around Mount Shasta near Weed become more and more dry, and the snow atop the big mountain disappeared earlier each year.

More importantly, we lived far enough upriver from the hordes in the valleys of California that fewer and fewer problems reached us. It became a time of peace as we settled into our way of life.

The years I spent alongside the upper Sacramento River turned into a time of blissful and fruitful endeavor. The younger people prospered and propagated, and soon a dozen children ran around the camp. I remember it as a time of peace, even though the temperatures remained high, the winds blew strong, and occasionally, the storms pelted our camp.

I turned forty-eight in 2063, and looking back on my life at that time, I felt I had experienced everything possible in life. Life had changed, but it seemed to have reached a consistent level. The wars were over. Constancy fell upon the land.

Little did I know at the time of the fortunes yet to befall me and our tribe.

The Puter said, "End of file."

The ProfSir said, "Class, we have just heard of the time of the greatest transition for the Great Collapse. This was when all the marvelous technology upon which that civilization depended fell away. Only those who had learned to live by the fruits of their own labors could survive. Remember this episode well.

He paused, then changed subjects. "Tomorrow we will continue to the north. It is a trip of nearly eighty klicks, so please be packed and ready to travel early."

Chapter 12: Claire

May 1, 2063

The archeological expedition moved another eighty klicks to the north alongside the Wilimit River to the shore across from the remains of Oregon City. Here lay the remains of the remaining concrete rock bridge that crossed the Wilimet River near the Great Columb River, an key bottleneck the troop faced in their journey home. Earlier explorations had found this to be the only path across the Wilimit.

They pitched the big tent and settled in to try to outlast the winds from the west. The ProfSir surveyed his troop. "You all did well today. Tomorrow we will cross the river using what remains of the broken bridge you all saw when we arrived.

"Tonight we hear of the time when the Sutherlin tribe lived on the upper reaches of the Sacramento River. They carried on communications with the rest of the globe using what they called satellites. These satellites circled the earth with transmitters and receivers in space that allowed various parts of the world to communicate with each other.

"It was during this time that this means of communications failed to work. At a Summer Solstice celebration to pray for its return, Sam met Claire. We will hear that she was the future mother of his sons, but her life was cut short."

CosandJo quickly said, "So Sam did have children. He can still be the father of our tribe. He could still be our roots."

ElderJan breathed a sigh and said, "CosandJo, you keep searching for your roots. Yes, it is possible, but we do not know. Be patient. Sam's sorrow at her passing is obvious from the shortness of this next chapter. Puter, please say to us the next file, Chap-12."

The Puter spoke, "The file says,"

In early 2063, while our tribe lived around the headwaters of the Sacramento and Shasta Rivers near Weed, I saw everything I knew to be our civilized society ending.

The crowning blow occurred in early 2064 when all the satellites ceased their signals. We could no longer see television or access the satellite Internet. The GPS no longer told us where we stood on the surface of the globe. The age of all that technology ended on the same day. Even my computer failed, though I did manage to restore it back to a functioning condition a few days later.

I learned later that a huge solar flare took out all of the space birds at the same time, along with most of electronics on the ground. The flare destroyed the surviving electrical network grid in the NAF. Those who depended upon non-local power sources had no power after the flare.

We spent several nights in February watching the Aurora Borealis light the nighttime sky above the top of Mount Shasta. The visions in the sky shined so beautifully; maybe because the weird, flashing streamers made no sound.

"Puter, please pause," said ProfSir ElderJan, wanting to comment on an important observation of that point in time.

"Much of the history we know tells of the great flock of space satellites used by the society before the Great Collapse for communications and control of their world. This passage from Sam's story confirms the extent to which they depended upon those facilities, and the catastrophe that struck their society when all systems failed.

"We must always remember that whenever we become too dependent upon a single resource, we are increasing our risk. Puter, please continue saying the file."

I dug out my old shortwave radio and tried it. Being one of the old windup types, I knew there would be no problem with the batteries.

In the beginning the static level hissed so loud I could hear nothing, another indication that a solar flare showered the earth with radiation. But in time the hiss began to subside, and I began to hear snatches of broadcasts from different places around the globe.

The first news report we could decipher from the static told of the havoc wrought by the destruction of all communications around the earth. They then said that the flow of the western Antarctica ice shelf had accelerated and more and more ice fell into the ocean. Much of the shelf entered the waters as icebergs and moved to the north. Sea levels increased worldwide by half a meter in the space of a month.

That summer what little electrical power our tribe produced began to fail more often in the enclave above Dunsmuir on the Sacramento River. The river often ran low, and our little turbine generators could not produce the level of power we needed, though some surviving solar and wind machines helped.

We became effective at communicating by shortwave radio with some of the other nearby enclaves, but we knew the point of total failure of our technology could not be far off. Whenever some critical piece broke, we often could not find a replacement, and we scrambled to find an alternative.

We spent much time on the radio trying to locate someone who made replacements for our failing technology, but we found no one. We even contacted some of the California state military units down south, but they told of even more problems than we had with finding spare parts and replacements.

For the summer solstice of 2064, the tribe planned a festival to pray for the return of our communications and a good crop and harvest. I am not sure who came up with the idea, but it seemed to be a good one. Everyone got into the swing of things and began planning for a great feast. Even I got sucked into the festive spirit.

At the celebration someone brought out a bottle of brew, something concocted from the grain and sugar beets we grew. It tasted much more potent than what I could ever believe possible in this new world of ours. Maybe then had found some plant extract to add to the juice. Trust the human race to reinvent such a marvel from the past.

After a couple of small sips, I remember dancing in the convivial circle with a garland of flowers around my neck. A young girl kept helping me dance, showing me the latest steps she and her friends had invented. She introduced herself as Claire.

"Why are you worrying with me?" I asked her.

"Because you are the most important man in our tribe, and I love you," she declared.

"Importance is no reason to love someone. I am an old dry husk, and you should be looking for a young sprout."

She laughed and swung me around in a circle as part of the dance. "Yes, but under that dry husk your seeds are strong." She took my hand and shook her body in gyrations. I tried to move my body in the same way, but it hurt. The booze in my head did not help.

"I watched you take a bath in the river. You are strong and you look beautiful." I blushed with surprise.

"What did you say your name was?"

"Claire."

I kept wondering what kind of dream world I stumbled into. I don't remember much more of that night.

The next morning, as I lay on my back on my mat, I dropped my right forearm across my brow and pressed down. It helped push some of the pain of the hangover away. Many years before I'd experienced my first and only hangover, but this one made up for all those missed opportunities.

I spread my left arm out to my side, and felt it encounter a soft, warm body. Turning my head, I saw a young female lying on her side facing me. I remember thinking, *She can't be more than sixteen. The tribe will have me before the council on a charge of child molestation.*

She breathed quietly in her slumber, her hand resting on my chest. Like me, she wore no clothes. As my mind came awake, I looked at the young girl more closely. She looked so familiar, and I finally realized she must be Claire from the night before. I reached out to grasp her shoulder and shook it.

"Claire, what are you doing here?" I whispered.

Her eyes opened, and she rolled toward me. She looked me in the eye and smiled. She murmured in reply, "Since I saw you in the river, I have loved you. I can see you are lonely. I want to take care of you." Then she closed her eyes and pulled her body next to mine in a warm embrace. I looked up into the blue sky above and wondered what else might have happened during the night.

It took several days to accept Claire's decision to adopt me and her refusal to leave. She began to care for me, feed me, and wash my clothes.

"You're only seventeen. I'm too old for you." I argued with her that she should return to her mother's home and search for someone younger to take care of, but she would not listen.

Each night she would come to sleep with me. In the beginning I ignored her and resisted the enticements of her body, but after three nights of fighting my urges, I gave in, and we made wild, passionate love. Memories of what it could be like returned from being buried in my mind after losing Abby.

Claire and I lived together for three months before she told me of her pregnancy. She was so happy, and I basked in her contagious excitement. I was forty-nine, but she was a healthy seventeen, so I did not expect there to be any problems. However, after checking with Marsha, I began to worry because childbirth had once again become one of the more dangerous occupations for the female gender. The medicines of the old times no longer existed, and now we depended upon midwives and sanitation to take care of those matters.

Claire worked in the fields with everyone else as her body grew. During the winter she helped sew skins into clothes for the baby. She ate like a horse whenever we could find food for her. She presented a picture of good health into the spring and early summer.

The morning of July 4, 2065, Claire went into labor and suffered horribly throughout the day. Marsha and Jill served as midwives and kept me busy boiling water and fetching other necessary items.

As the sun set, Claire presented me with twin sons. I named them Jeremiah and Joseph. They came into life with red, frizzy hair and tiny tails. A wave of happiness flooded through me as I considered being a father, but I wondered at the kind of world these two boys would see.

Then disaster struck. An embolism that would have presented no real problem when my mother birthed me in 2015 became a fatal affliction to a young woman of 2065, and Claire died four days later. Our tribe possessed no medicines to heal the wounds, nothing to fight the infections. We used some weeds and herbs to fight the pain, but they could not cure the cause. I had lost Claire, but gained two sons.

######### \\\\\\\\\

The Puter said, "End of file."

CosandJo asked, "ProfSir, didn't they use the herbal medicines we use? Why did Claire die?"

"The society of the twenty-first century had grown away from using the remedies of nature as their technology advanced. They depended upon manufactured medicines, and lost much of their natural immunity to diseases. Their health system became too complicated. It took many years for our ancestors to relearn the fundamentals of our medical system."

CosandJo asked a second question, "But why did Claire get pregnant in the first place? Didn't they understand how to control such things?"

"That also became too complicated, and then maybe Claire wanted her babies. They managed the world back then much less than we manage ours today."

The class sat in silence, thinking about how far their tribe had come from that time. The ProfSir rose and left them to their thoughts.

Chapter 13: Raising Twins

July 4, 2065

The archeological expedition crossed the big bridge over the Wilimet River the next day. Parts of the bridge lay in the water, but enough remained that by walking single file and guiding their cycles behind them, the troop made it without incident.

When they gathered on the other side, ProfSir ElderJan said, "That is enough excitement for the day. We will set up our tent on the clear area ahead and stay here for three days to explore the remains of Oregon City. This is part of the large population center called Port Land. We know it survived for a while after the Great Collapse, but like other cities of that time, it died.

"There are some natives in this area, so be careful when you explore. I believe them to be friendly, but do not take a chance. Only go in groups—no one should venture out on their own."

After raising the tent and sending the students out to look for treasures, the ProfSir readied the tent for the reading from the Puter that evening. During the day several groups brought back strange remains from the civilization that lived there a thousand years before. ElderJan helped them catalog the items and made notes on their possible uses.

The group had their evening meal and arranged themselves for the next reading of Sam Hardy's memoirs.

ProfSir ElderJan nodded appreciation for the organization and said, "Puter, please say to us the next file, Chap-13."

After Claire died, my cousin Marsha and her daughter Jill moved into my house to help raise the boys. Life proved to be a struggle, and we almost lost both twins until one of the tribe's goats birthed a kid and Jill could steal milk to feed the babies. We made quite a family, all with flaming red hair and big bones. I often cried myself to sleep thinking about their mother, taken at such a young age by the mere absence of the medical help available only a few years before.

I learned how to be a father, and in time the boys grew into toddlers. They were small bundles of energy. If that had been all that life held, it would have been a delightful episode, but as we lost contact with the rest of civilization, once again savages came out of the hinterlands and began to attack our tribe.

It was difficult raising my sons in that environment, but with continuing help and advice from Marsha and Jill, I made it through. We decided in mid-2067, when the boys turned two, that we must teach them everything we ever learned to be sure they survived in this new world. And we must teach them things we did not even know ourselves.

Though the Internet had died a few years before, I still ran some games on the old computer I somehow kept going at that time. I decided to use the games as instructional tools to sharpen the boy's minds. I had kept copies of old Wiki articles on all my favorite subjects stored away on discs, and we could draw on a wealth of information, though it most often told of a world that had long since died. But at least the information gave the boys some ideas for possibilities.

I did not take into account that the boys inherited the mental mutations blessed upon me from my father's family, for they learned far faster and understood far more than I actually taught them. They surprised me when they began to read on their own before they turned three.

Over time I built a curriculum to use with my sons, and started bringing in other children from our tribe for the lessons. I built a class of twenty students that ranged in ages from three to seventeen.

I found that my first task with the new kids involved teaching each one to read. Most of the other parents could not read, for they and their parents grew up in a world revolving around the social networking communications, more visual and verbal than written. To absorb the information left in the books and Wiki articles, the children must be able to read.

Being an engineer, I wanted to stress the laws of physics, chemistry, and math, but Marsha and Jill pushed back and said the curriculum should also focus on the practical matters of life, like the principles of farming and animal husbandry. We agreed on a mix.

Marsha let me take responsibility for the science section. I found chemistry the hardest thing to teach because a supply of raw materials for the basic experiments of chemistry did not exist. Much of our study focused on how to separate the various elements and compounds needed for chemistry from the common materials around us.

Jill expanded our chemistry studies by showing things that could be done with plants and animal remains. For instance, she worked out the chemistry of fertilizing plants with urine and cattle and horse dung.

The studies of mathematics proved more interesting, and my boys really enjoyed it. Many articles in my collection from Wiki covered different parts of mathematics, but we lived in a world where one could find few if any practical applications for the mathematics. So math became more of a mental game than a practical tool.

I devised a number of experiments in physics, especially on the use of forces and levers, to illustrate the use of mathematics. This also laid the groundwork for a good understanding for the mechanics of tools and surveying.

Jill taught the children martial arts, woodcraft, and horsemanship. Her natural ability when it came to working with any of our livestock proved phenomenal. She took special pride in the practice of animal husbandry, and she taught the subject as a matter of practical genetic selection and helping the stock raise their young. She started a long-term experiment with ways to improve our farm animals by controlling the intermingling of the herds.

Marsha turned out to be the best farmer among us. The study of farming involved understanding the kinds of plants that could be raised in various environments. It also considered the need for controlled variations in the planting schedules. Marsha had a natural affinity for what would grow where. I remembered how thirty years before the old farming methods focused on monoculture crops and massive amounts of artificial fertilizer, and how those methods had destroyed much of the farmland in the Midwest.

Our local communication system no longer worked. An intermittent radiophone system served us for years, and we listened to radio communications with the outside world, but the ravages of time took its toll and more and more of the electronic components failed. I realized that the lack of communication with the rest of society made it harder and harder to organize to repel the invaders. It foretold the end of our peaceful life.

When I realized the fragility of our system, I immediately began a crash course on electronics. But of course, we had no computer or communications chips readily available, nor soldering irons to build circuits. Instead, the students learned how to salvage electronics and make do with what we could find.

I explained the natural phenomena of weather to the class. We needed to predict the weather for the next day or week, but also for the coming years. The heat increase had become terrible, and the Sacramento River valley looked like a desert. People camped around the Sacramento River reservoir but as the water dried up, they found few fish and little food. At least they could draw water. Even the upper reaches of the Sacramento Valley where we lived grew increasingly dry.

I explained to the children the world we lived in, how it developed, and how it could be expected to change. I taught history and told of the faraway tribes on the other continents and explained what happened to them.

We taught other subjects as the opportunities presented themselves. One day Joey asked in the middle of the class, "Why do Jerry and I have a tail, and the other kids don't?"

I sort of laughed and maybe even blushed, then explained, "You two have a tail because I have a tail. I found out I had a tail because my dad had a tail. It is called a genetic trait that runs in our family."

Jerry volunteered, "Aunt Marsha and Cousin Jill both have tails. They showed us."

The rest of the class laughed, and I tried to control the leap into genetics. "Look, this is one of the traits of the Hardy family, to have tails. I don't know why we need to have a tail, but that is the way we are. Most other humans do not have tails. It is a mutation that started in our family at least two generations ago, and that is the way it is. There is nothing wrong with it, but there is also nothing special about it either."

"Puter, pause here." The ProfSir shifted his body into a more comfortable position.

"Class, when I first heard this passage in Sam's story, I realized that this is the truest evidence that Sam and his family are part of our ancestry. We all have tails, and it is a unique genetic mutation that ties us all together. It is our test for being a Neu-human."

CosandJo said, "So Sam may not be our direct ancestor, but he is part of the tribe from which we are descended. Is that right?"

"Yes, that is a logical conclusion that can be made. We may not have found our literal roots, but we found a very early part of our family and tribe. You can be proud of that accomplishment."

He continued, "We do know from our oral history that for a time during the twenty-second and twenty-third centuries our tribe very nearly died. Some call it the "time of the bottle-neck," but I am not sure what that means. Our tribal numbers approached the level of extinction. The few that survived that period are the primary ancestors of our people today, and it appears they probably derived from Sam's family in the Oregon Lands."

The rest of the class grunted their recognition of this news. The implications moved them.

The ProfSir said, "Puter, please continue."

The schooling project took place over several years as the boys grew. We used other learning activities to occupy their time. For instance, I remember when I decided to teach the class to catch fish.

When I grew up as a boy my dad bought fishing poles, monofilament fishing line, and metal hooks for us to use in the Sacramento River. I told how I fished back then, and they could only imagine it. I said, "Now we must create our own gear, and a fishing gig will be a better implement. We will use it to spear the fish."

I explained how to make a fishing gig from a long thin pole with the multipronged, barbed gig at the end. I salvaged some heavy metal wire from the ruins around Weed. "We could make a gig with wood or bone, but it easier to work with this copper. It will stay sharper much longer, and we can pound it to re-sharpen it."

I showed the boys and girls how to cut a piece of wire about a foot long. Then we pounded and sharpened one end of the wire to a point, folded an inch back on itself, and pounded the bend into another sharp point, leaving the first end sticking out to act as a barb. We made three of the barbed points.

Next I showed the children how to attach the barbed points to the end of the fishing pole by wrapping smaller wire around the pole and points and pulling it tight. Jerry asked me, "Why don't we use sinew from the deer the tribe killed two days ago? It is a lot easier and shrinks when it dries."

"Yes, but when sinew gets wet again, it relaxes and expands, and we could lose our points," I explained. "This tool is for fishing, and we must get it wet to catch fish."

We walked down to the river and found a large rock next to a deep pool. The water of the northern Sacramento River flowed clear and smooth, and if we sat still we could see several good-sized trout swimming several feet under the water. "Now, watch me fish with our new gig." I slowly placed the pole into the water and lowered it to where fish swam by earlier. "See how the pole seems to bend where it enters the water. That is called refraction. You must adjust where you point your gig because the fish will not be where it appears to be if you think in a straight line. Now we sit still and wait."

After what seemed to be a long, long time, one of the fish came back into the area of the gig. I watched as it swam under the points, then quickly thrust down, driving the points into the fish. "And here comes our supper." I lifted the fish from the water and put it over next to the group.

"I want to do it now." Jerry scrambled up to take my place on the rock. That afternoon the class caught five more trout. They made a good meal for the tribe that evening.

As my boys grew older, Jill began a regimen of classes on the finer arts of warfare. She taught all the boys and girls the basic skills of hand-to-hand combat. She developed a troop of stick carriers who used seven foot long, one-and-a-half inch diameter wooden shafts to lay waste to any assailant they could find. Most often, that would be a weed thicket or a grove of small trees, but one day they came upon a black momma bear and her two cubs. By the time the assault finished, Jill's students provided the tribe with a rack of bear meat and three fine pelts.

Jill's army began doing close-order drills and developed maneuvers, plans, and strategies for various situations she could think of. They would take the top of a hill from imaginary invaders, and then defend it from the returning hordes.

I asked her one day, "Why are you doing this? You've created an army, but there is no enemy out there now."

"Sam," she replied, "I think we simply bought some time by moving north to this location. Those hordes you defeated in the south still breed, and they are still hungry. We are one of the wealthiest tribes in this area in terms of food and tools. We are the target, and the word will get out that we are here. We must be ready. They will come."

Her words became a prophecy. In the spring of 2076 a lone scout from the southland crept into our area and came upon my son Joseph working in the maize field. Ten-year-old Joey had laid his wooden staff on the ground at the beginning of the row of grain stalks, and he bent over to pluck weeds from around the plants. His daydreaming meant he did not sense the savage running toward him with a raised knife until almost too late.

Jill's training in hand-to-hand combat saved Joey's life, for he rolled over and pitched the savage over his head with his feet. Jumping up, he ran to retrieve his staff, and as the savage returned with his knife-hand raised, Joey swung his staff and caught the intruder in the side of his ribcage. The attacker fell into the field of maize with four broken ribs. Joey brought his pole up over the fallen savage and brought its base down on the gnarly head, splitting his skull.

Joey's shout brought other members of the tribe to the field, and one came back to fetch me. Outraged that I came so close to losing my son, I quickly organized a posse, and we backtracked the savage until we found his family camped downriver from our settlement. We killed them all.

But the danger remained. Once again our homes had become unsafe in an unsafe land. I knew in my heart that the upper Sacramento Valley would soon be swept into savage wars with the southern hordes. A predatory life became the necessary way to live as supplies ran out in various parts of the country and the horde of savages emerged from the former urban areas in the south to go out to take what others possessed.

A few weeks later, I strung several pieces of old cloth around our campfire area and prepared for a party. First the children and then the adults gathered around to watch me, wondering what the old man could have in mind.

Marsha and Jill came out to help as we prepared small bits of food and placed them on sticks at various points around the fire pit.

When we had the area ready, I climbed atop one of the larger rocks and looked around at my tribe. "You people of the Tribe of Jakes, come join me, for today is July 4, 2076. Today we celebrate my twin sons' eleventh birthday, and it is also the three hundredth anniversary of the Declaration of Independence of the United States of America.

"Sit around the fire pit and partake of the food bites we prepared." The group slowly came to the area and seated themselves around the pit. A few and then more picked up the morsels and ate.

One in the group asked, "What is the Declaration of Independence?"

I explained, "Three hundred years ago, a group of early settlers to this continent declared their freedom and independence from the control of the kings who lived in Europe. They declared their independence in a new land, and they said they would thereafter rule their own lives. It was those people who founded our society."

"But that doesn't make any difference anymore."

I looked directly at the woman who spoke. "Yes, it does make a difference even now. We are still free to choose what we want to be and where we want to go. This Declaration of Independence remains part of our life. I declare that this tribe will celebrate Independence Day on July 4 of each year so long as I am leader of this tribe."

I smiled and added, "Besides, today is my sons' birthday. Let us celebrate."

"End of file," the Puter said.

CosandJo eyes grew bright and almost teary, "We celebrate Independence Day on July 4 each year, just like Sam's tribe did. That is more proof we must be related."

The ProfSir smiled, "Yes, it would seem that is one tradition that our ancestors carried down for over a thousand years. It is good to have traditions like that."

CHAPTER 14: FORCED INTO OREGON

APRIL 30, 2077

The ProfSir sat upon his pillow and said, "Everyone worked well today, and our supply of treasures continues to grow. However, most of the items found are things we have seen before and are already represented in the university museum.

"It is now time for us to hear the next episode in the saga of Sam Hardy. We will hear how his tribe lived along the upper reaches of the Sacramento River for several years, but pressures from the savages living in the lands to the south grew, and he began to look for a way out."

MeJe said, "But I thought Sam had waged war on those that were harassing his tribe, and that ended the problem."

ElderJan answered, "It reduced the problem for a time, but those to the south bred rapidly, and there were soon more people than that land could support. The problem returned. But let us hear of this from Sam. Puter, please say to us the file, Chap-14."

In 2077 my family provided the major part of the leadership of the Jakes tribe living alongside the origins of the Sacramento River in northern California. We had moved north to the area around Weed several years before to escape the encroaching hordes, but some of us realized we must find a way to move even further north to protect ourselves from the savagery that engulfed the southlands. The events surrounding our move to Oregon will tell you much of the status of northern California in the late 2070s.

The poor, starving people who came out of the Mexican and southern California ghettos, those who survived the multiple epidemics that swept the region, made up the hordes I am talking about. The NAF government tried for years to support them, but over time sufficient energy and food could not be found to sustain their existence. Like locusts, they spread across the land searching for provisions, parasites on those who had learned survival methods.

Now the migrants from the south had us cornered. Nothing but mountains lay to the north of us—we had run out of farmland and defensible space.

The original Jakes tribe that settled alongside the larger Sacramento River, south of the remains of the ghost town of Redding numbered about seven hundred, and we had a good supply of livestock to support our operations, including horses, cows, goats, and chickens.

We believed we had solved the problems of the southern hordes in the Sacramento River Wars of 2051, but experience proved us wrong. The hordes kept breeding and more and more savages came from the south.

As the pressure rebuilt, a majority of the Jakes moved to Weed, but even that was not far enough.

During the late winter rains of 2077, my cousin, Marsha, and I looked over the old road maps of the western United States that the tribe had collected over time. She asked, "Sam, you told me you went to Oregon one time. What do you know about the area? Can we find a place there with water and land to farm? And are there enough mountains to protect us from the hordes?"

I scratched my graying chin whiskers, a sure sign of my sixty-two years. "When I was a kid, Dad took me on the train up to Sutherlin, Oregon, to visit my great-grandparents. They took us over to Reedsport on the Oregon coast, about sixty miles west. I remember grandpa drove his old truck along the Umpqua River, and it ran a pretty good stream in the middle of summer, so I expect anywhere along there should be a good place to live. It is remote, so there wouldn't be as much of a problem with the hordes as we have down here. Reedsport should be a good fishing village, even now."

"Why don't you check it out?" she asked. "Maybe that is the place our tribe should go."

Jill came in from the fields with my eight-year-old twin sons, Joey and Jerry, in tow and reported, "We just caught a couple more vagrants trying to break into the tomato patch veggie house. They really stunk."

Jill, a tall fifty-one-year-old with a waist-length ponytail of reddish-gray hair, pounded her fist onto the table to emphasize how she handled the problem. "I hit 'em alongside the head and threw them into the river and let them float down stream. I doubt they'll be back soon." Jill had grown into a big, looming woman, and I felt pity for whoever she hit alongside the head.

My son, Joey, puffed his chest and added, "I hit 'em, too, right across their knees with my stick. I made sure they won't come back."

Jerry pushed Joey aside. "He didn't need to do that. Aunt Jill had knocked them out cold. But they sure did stink."

Marsha looked her daughter in the eye and said, "Jill, somehow we've got to get away from the kind of trash that's drifting into these parts. What do you think about you and Sam taking a trip north to explore the Oregon coast and finding a new place for us to live? I can stay here to watch the kids, and other members of the tribe can clear out the vagrants."

Jill showed surprise at her mother's suggestion, but she looked at me and asked, "What about you, Sam? Think you and I can travel far enough together to do any good without getting into an argument?" Our constant bickering had become a standing joke in the tribe over the years.

"Sure, that is, if your mother will give me written authority to keep you in line. And with you along, I won't need help from anyone else." Jill stuck out her tongue at me as Marsha laughed.

Two months later, in late April of 2077, Jill and I loaded two packhorses with a small stash of food and extra clothing, saddled two of our better riding horses, and headed south down the Sacramento. We passed Dunsmuir and came to the shores of Shasta Lake. Amazingly, the old I-5 roadway still existed, along with the bridges that crossed the arms of the lake.

I did not want to venture into the Redding town limits. I expected we would find too many of the riffraff from the south in that area, so we headed west, toward the old town of Shasta. The broken pavement wound past the few houses and business buildings that remained of those that had fallen, leaving only a few weeds and vine-covered walls.

Our clothing was a mix of homespun and leather, with a few remnants we dug out of trunks in the abandoned houses back near the river. Jill's bow and a quiver of arrows hung across her shoulders, and she propped a steel-tipped lance in a pocket alongside her stirrup.

I carried a rusted but imposing-looking long-barrel 12-gauge shotgun over the pommel of my saddle. I carried only three shells in my coat pocket, but no one would know that. My crossbow hung from my belt. Both of us also had good strong hunting knives strapped around our waists.

A few solitary settlers waved us on, but none offered to speak with us. The solitary ones would trade with the tribe from time to time, but they wanted to remain independent. I worried that if the hordes moved north in earnest, those people would be overrun before they could defend themselves. Their fate would not be a nice one, but they had made their choice.

Further along, we passed a few small junipers and lots of weeds and grass alongside the roadbed, but few signs of structures. I told Jill, "I remember a big fire went through here a few years ago." I pointed ahead. "Look, there's an old metal sign lying beside the road. It says Shasta."

Late in the afternoon, after winding up the side of a long hill, we rode through a road-cut and looked out over a large lake. "Where did that come from?" Jill exclaimed. "I didn't even know it existed." We guided our horses to a flat area that at one time must have been an observation point alongside the road.

I pulled out the old roadmap I had brought along. "The map says this must be Whiskeytown Lake. It's manmade." I pointed south. "You can see the dam over there. I think it feeds Cottonwood Creek when water runs over the spillway. I know there's a tribe near the headwaters of the Cottonwood, and this must be their source of water and power. Guess they have some hydroelectric turbines they have not talked about because from time to time they seem to have electricity."

"Won't the dam break?" Jill asked.

"I suppose it will sometime in the future, but it takes many years for erosion to eat away the foundations of a structure like this."

Jill looked around. "We've traveled almost twenty miles since this morning. Isn't that far enough for a day's ride? Let's camp here. It's flat with a good field of fire if someone should attack us." I nodded and went down the slope to search for firewood by the lakeshore while Jill hobbled the horses. I returned with a few sticks of dried wood, and using my piezoelectric-starter, I soon had a small flame burning in a mat of dried leaves. We built a larger fire in a cavity in the rocks.

I had seen a juniper bush along the ride and had broken off some sprigs. I dropped those springs into a quart pot of water that we heated to make tea. We drank our tea and ate a small handful of dried grapes and seeds. It soothed our hunger for one night, but we would need something more for sustenance the next day. "Use that monofilament you found to set out some snares," I said to Jill. "Maybe we can catch breakfast."

The next morning, as the sky turned from black to a dark blue and then pale yellow, we found a couple of cottontail rabbits caught in our snares. Jill clubbed them behind the ears, stripped off their skin, disemboweled them, and speared them on sticks while I restarted our fire for roasting our meat. I rubbed them with salt and rosemary and placed them over our little bed of embers.

"Scrape out those skins," I said. "We'll find some use for them later on this trip."

After watering the horses at the lake, we repacked our gear, re-saddled the horses, and set off west alongside the lake. I could see a few people fishing from boats out on the water. It appeared most of them lived on the other side of the lake. Again, they seemed reluctant to interact with us—after all, they did not know us.

We followed the winding roadbed and camped at the top of the pass above Whiskeytown. The next day we rode down into the Trinity River valley. As we approached the riverbed, I could see very little water in the stream, and no current flowed.

"Why do you think the river's dry?" asked Jill.

"As the map showed, the Trinity River is dammed up above here, and I think most of its water is sent through a tube to Whiskeytown Lake. That's the reason the lake was so full. But by doing that, there's no water left to flow down the main channel of the Trinity, so it's dry most of the time.

With no one left to control the flow, it requires a flood before something comes down this way."

"It looks awful." Jill echoed my feelings, looking at the corpse of a magnificent river.

I told her in consolation, "But someday, those dams and tubes will fail. Then nature will return the flows to the levels from the past."

We camped near the place where the road crossed the bed of the Trinity River. We made a dry camp with no water, even though the plants declared it to be springtime.

The next morning I looked at the map. "See how the road leaves the river just below here? It goes up through the old town of Weaverville, then over the pass to rejoin the river at Junction City. We could follow the river, but I think we should go with the road."

The horses made good time up the old roadbed, and we soon entered the outskirts of Weaverville. Another monstrous fire had swept through the area and destroyed most of the town. We saw no evidence of anyone living there. All of the wells and streams had dried up, leaving a wasteland.

After a brief rest, we hustled our horses up the next hill and over the pass, then back down to the Trinity River. Scars of hydraulic mining for gold from the nineteenth century could still be seen alongside the roads.

When we reached the river, we found a small amount of water flowing in the riverbed. Some upstream creeks fed the river. We reached the area identified as Junction City and camped next to the small Canyon Creek coming down the slope from the east.

"The creek is putting enough water into the river for there to be some fish. Give me a length of that monofilament and I'll catch supper," I said.

Jill pulled about ten feet off her roll and cut it off. "This should be enough if you're any good."

"Watch this." I waded into the willows alongside the river and found a long stem. Cutting it at the base, I cleaned off the leaves and twigs and tied the end of the plastic line around the end of the branch. Reaching into my back pocket, I took out a small plastic pouch containing a small fish hook and a string of black yarn. I attached the hook to the line and wrapped the yarn around the top of the hook.

"Where did you get that?"

"I always carry fishing supplies. In case I get hungry." I looked at Jill and smiled. "Now, we're dealing with a fish that never ever saw a hook or artificial lure. Just watch this." I tossed the yarn-covered hook seven feet out into the white water of the creek.

To my extreme surprise, the water exploded as a fish of immense proportions leapt from the water to gobble the bait into its mouth. My immediate problem became one of trying to land a much larger fish than I had expected. What a thrill. With ten feet of line and a springy willow pole, I fought the fish downstream into calmer water and, with Jill's help, beached it on the bank.

"Wow. That fish must be three feet long and weigh fifteen pounds. What is it?"

I bent down and clasped my knees. "That, my dear, is a steelhead." My breath came easier now that we had landed the fish, and I looked at it with admiration. "Grandpa told me about them, and he even showed me a picture of one from a book he had, but he said they had all died off."

That evening, I fixed a big strong fire and we baked the fish in the coals. What a glorious meal.

The next day we continued on down the Trinity River toward the area the map labeled as Big Bar. We stopped for the night after about fifteen miles, where we found some grass for the horses. Our supper of leftover steelhead is still a great memory.

The following day we made another twenty miles and reached the area called Burnt Ranch, in the deep canyon of the Trinity River. I worried that the road had fallen over time, but we found the path to be clear.

Sixteen miles the next day brought us to the settlement of Willow Creek. Four miles upstream from the town, the south fork of the Trinity joined the north fork we had been following, and it provided a significant flow of water. The Trinity once again flowed like a real river.

We found an encampment of about seventy-five souls at Willow Creek. After we introduced ourselves and explained our journey, they welcomed us into their homes. They called themselves the South Hoopa Tribe and traced their ancestry to the Hoopa Indian Reservation located downstream from Willow Creek on the Trinity River.

The chief, Big Joe Smith, was the biggest man I had ever seen. I stood at six foot five, and I looked up another six inches to see into his eyes. Jill smiled standing next to him, her size diminished by his dimensions. She told me she felt smaller than she ever had felt before.

Big Joe explained, "When things started going bad in the world, and gasoline and kerosene became so expensive, my parents said to hell with it and moved back to the reservation down at Hoopa. The government paid us a stipend for a number of years, but that stopped when the Indian Agent died of the flu. We haven't had any representation since, and we don't want it. We get along with nature the way it is. We just went back to being Indians."

Jill asked, "What do you eat?"

"What we always ate before civilization came along and messed things up. Salmon and steelhead and some maize we grow. When they could not find enough fuel for the commercial fishing boats to go out into the ocean and destroy the salmon, the fish started coming back. We get big runs now, along with some nice steelhead."

"Do you eat anything else?" I asked.

Big Joe laughed. "Oh yes, along with the grain that we raise along the river, there are some good veggie farms where they grow potatoes and tomatoes and some other stuff. We also heard a few animals like goats, pigs, cattle, and chickens, but most of our meat comes from the fish. The good thing is we aren't bothered by many people coming around and snooping on us. The roads are blocked unless you're afoot or on a horse. It's so much better than it was before."

"Have you seen any of the savages from the south?"

Big Joe pursed his brow and replied, "A couple of crazies came through here last year, and they talked about hordes of people back where they came from. Said those people were starving and doing crazy things.

"Then they made the mistake of stealing food from one of the families and fondling their girl. It didn't take long. Those nutcases are fish food now, but don't tell anyone I told you that. We just don't put up with that sort of thing around here." He looked at me with a stern visage, as if warning me that I should not get out of line.

I nodded. "I know how you feel, but you better worry about those hordes. In time, they may start to come over this way." I explained to him, "The problem is that what's left of most of the people of California have no food or roots. They are living off the land and anything else they can find. The reason Jill and I are traveling this way is we figure we must move our tribe out of their path. We need to find some place where we can live in peace. And it is not in the big valley of California."

We stayed three days with the South Hoopa Tribe, and Jill received two marriage proposals, one from Big Joe. She blushed, but said no. I was glad. I did not want to continue the journey alone. Then I saw Jill pull Big Joe aside and whisper in his ear. I wondered.

That night I talked with Big Joe about continuing down the Trinity to the Klamath River, or heading west to the coast. He suggested that the route going to the coast would be safer. The road through the Trinity canyon below Hoopa had fallen away from the canyon walls, making that path close to impassable.

Next morning at daybreak the ground began shaking from an earthquake. The vibrations grew in strength for over two minutes, knocking down some of the wooden huts of the Hoopas but doing little other damage to the surroundings.

I learned later that what we felt had been the rupture of the Cascadia sub-duction zone from southern Oregon up to Puget Sound in Washington. That earthquake launched a series of tsunamis that wiped the coast of Oregon and Washington clean. Jill and I would find the effects of that event throughout out travels over the next six months.

ProfSir ElderJan said, "Stop a moment, Puter." He paused for a moment of silence.

"Class, we know from several other sources that two great earthquakes happened on this continent in the twenty-first century: one in the middle of the country called the Second New Madrid, and one on the west coast called the Seattle Tsunami Quake. These two seismic events did terrible damage to the society and civilization of the North American continent because of the population distributions and pressures. And it appears their scientists expected both but the people made little preparation for them."

SueJu asked, "Have there been large earthquakes since that time?"

ElderJan nodded. "Oh yes, earthquakes occur regularly in the same seismic zones. But they damage much less because there is so much less to damage. One of the things we must remember is that nature will always change things over time. Our race is the big variable. Puter, please continue."

On the morning of our fifth day in Willow Creek, the first of May, Jill and I again saddled our horses and headed west along the old U.S. 299 roadbed. We traveled a hilly country with no water. We made a dry camp halfway to the coast and rode into the coastal town of Blue Lake the next day.

Blue Lake sat two hundred feet above sea level and upstream on the Mad River behind a narrow canyon that protected it from the violence of the sea tsunami. When the waves hit two days earlier, there had been a rush of refugees into the small valley, followed by a gush of water up the canyon. The towns of Eureka and Arcata had been wiped from the map along with those who could not outrun the waters rushing up the slopes.

Jill and I rode our horses and towed our pack animals west to the old Highway 101, looking at the ruins along the coast. We saw no way we could help anyone, so we continued on despite the pleas from the refugees along the way. The immense devastation continued for miles.

At last, when we reached Trinidad twenty-five miles further on, we escaped the tragic smell of death. We spent the night there on the side of a hill high above the sound of the pounding Pacific surf.

We rode past Big Lagoon, Stone Lagoon, and Freshwater Lagoon. The devastation in the areas near sea level matched that in Eureka. The little town of Orick on Redwood Creek lay flat, and no one seemed to be around.

The road turned into the mountains, and we left sight of the coast. It felt good to be away from that place, and the forests showed little damage. But when we reached the bridge over the Klamath River, we faced our first real obstacle. The bridge no longer stood above the river—it lay in the river channel.

Others looked for a way across the river. Several hundred people milled around the base of the old bridge, looking to see if it would rise from the waters. They did not seem to know what to do.

As the tide slackened, Jill and I lightened our packs and saddles and drove the horses into the stream above the bridge. Swimming alongside, we led them across the river, and a mile downstream found a spot where we could bring them ashore.

After drying out, we headed past the broken town of Requa and on up Highway 101. After a few miles, we came over the hill and looked toward the site of Crescent City. The city no longer existed. Again we camped, waiting until morning before venturing into the remains of the urban center.

We could see the signs of the great devastation of the earthquake and the tsunami. The city suffered from a tsunami in 1964 from the Alaskan earthquake. Now the tsunami from the 2077 Cascade earthquake cleared the land for one to three miles back from the coast. We saw very few people alive in the area, all the way from Crescent City to Smith River.

The destruction continued north along the coast to Pelican Beach. When we reached Brookings, Oregon, we found the area totally destroyed.

We continued up the coast of Oregon. The tsunami waves had wiped out every establishment that had been within fifty feet of sea level, and the people who had survived still showed signs of shock.

The bridges over the rivers and bays most often remained standing, but they had been strained by the pressures from the water. However, the harbors and towns had been scrubbed clean by the tsunami waters, and most of the population had disappeared.

Most of Port Orford had been destroyed as the waves swept over and around the beaches and hills of sand protecting the area. The Elk River basin had become a wasteland, along with the beaches and sand dunes to the north to Bandon.

The outer reaches around Coos Bay had been wiped by the waves, but the interior bay escaped much of the damage. However, the bridges no longer spanned the bay. We turned inland to get around Coos Bay and continued our journey to the north.

We worked our way up the coast to the area around Winchester Bay. It too had been cleansed by the waves. Much of the town of Reedsport had been inundated, but the upper part of the town survived. We found a few people who lived in the area, and they intended to stay there. However, they had no idea how they would survive.

By this time it was the middle of May. We stayed in the area for two weeks, looking over the possibilities for our tribe to move to the area. We found some good lands for farming, and the fishing possibilities looked excellent. The bay appeared to be in good shape, and with most everything wiped clean by the tsunami it presented many opportunities for developing the kind of place we wanted.

About the first of June, Jill and I turned inland, heading to where the old town of Roseburg sat and where the old I-5 roadway crossed the Umpqua River. The remains of the road up the river to Sutherlin remained passable on horseback, though landslides almost blocked our path in several places. Turning south on I-5, we made our way over the Sextons and into Grants Pass and the Rogue valley.

We crossed Siskiyou Pass the middle of June and went down into Weed. We arrived home on July 4, 2077. It was good to be back.

Marsha told me that while we were gone the attacks grew worse from the hordes, but nothing important happened. I told her of some of our experiences, and we arranged that there would be a tribal meeting the next night for Jill and me to report.

The next night the tribe gathered around a roaring fire. Jill and I told of our journey and what we saw, and then I made my recommendations.

I told the tribe, "The land along the coast is devastated, first by the epidemics and then by the earthquake and tsunami. At this time it is a wasteland, but within a year or two it will be returning to normal. The strongest earthquakes happened and will not return for hundreds of years. Nor will the tsunamis wipe the land. It is a land ready for us to take over, and the people who lived there are scattered and alone. They will welcome our coming to their land and rebuilding. Now is the time we must move to the Oregon coast."

Bob, an elder from the old tribe, stood and said, "But, Sam, this is our home. This is where we built our future. We cannot leave this area."

"Bob," I said. "This is my home as well, and it has been a good home. But now we are once again facing the hordes from the south, and they are marching toward us like locusts. They will overrun us and destroy us if we stay here. Our only hope is to move to a safer area. I believe we are forced to move to the Oregon coast."

"No, no, we must stay here. We must fight these hordes and push them back. They cannot be that strong." Bob looked over the other tribe members. "Raise your hands if you want to stay with me in our homes." Over half the tribe lifted their hands, and I could see that most of the people in the tribe had set their roots too deep in the lands along the upper Sacramento River to leave.

"Bob, I understand how you and many others want to stay, but some of us think we must leave and go to Oregon. Do you object? May we go?"

Bob looked perplexed. "If that is the way you feel, Sam, you must go. But we will not come to help you. You will be on your own."

So began preparation for the great exodus of my family to Oregon.

By the following spring in 2078, the raids and atrocities became too much. A group of us numbering forty-nine packed to leave, and we headed west, retracing our explorations toward the coast. I turned sixty-six, but I still had my health, and the younger people allowed me to go along.

My sons Joey and Jerry took responsibility for me.

We wandered through the wilderness over to the Trinity and then to the coast where Eureka once stood. We turned north along the coast and lived off the land.

One of the losses we experienced on the trip happened when we went through Willow Creek again. This time Jill told Marsha and me she would stay with Big Joe. "I never found a real man before. He is what I looked for all my life." We would miss her.

We camped along the coast as we moved slowly to the north. It took another year before my family and tribe reached our next home on the Umpqua River in Oregon. We settled in Winchester, just south of Reedsport, Oregon.

The Puter spoke, "End of file Chap-14," and went silent.

ElderJan said, "It is amazing that so few of the original tribe wanted to move on. We know from other historical accounts that the situation south of the Oregon Lands became terrible and chaotic during that time, and a huge die-off of people of that society ensued. This feature of unwillingness to adjust for the inevitable seems to be a common feature of the society of the past."

CosandJo asked, "Are we Neu-humans still unwilling to adjust and accept what is coming about?"

"No, part of the genetic changes in the Neu-humans appears to be a much more rational approach to what is happening. It is a willingness to accept reality for fact rather than seeing only what is desired. As a result, we are proactive in our responses."

CHAPTER 15: NEW REEDSPORT

JULY 4, 2084

The ProfSir positioned himself on his pillows and addressed the assembled class. "You have done well in your searches of this part of the Oregon Lands and have found some artifacts that we will study this fall when we return to the university. DanJa, you met one of the local natives. Please tell us of your experience."

DanJa stood to talk to the class. "MeJe and I were walking through what appeared to be one of the old neighborhoods away from the river. There were a few mounds where shelters may have once stood, and there were a few concrete remains scattered about in the grass.

"As we walked into a small grove of trees, we came upon a child, maybe five years in age. He was picking berries and putting them into a woven basket, though he popped every other one he picked into his mouth. He was startled when we appeared, and his eyes were wide. I should mention his hair was almost white, and he wore only a loin cloth.

MeJe interrupted, "He started talking to us in a language we could not understand, though it had some old Aenglish words mixed in."

DanJa cast MeJe a look of disapproval for the interruption and continued. "We said hello, and he turned and ran back into the brush. Apparently we frightened him in some way.

"We were not sure if he had gone to find his parents or other natives, so we decided to hurry back to camp. Our job was to find treasure, not to make contact with the natives."

ElderJan nodded his head. "You made the right decision. You may have been safe, but you never know. I have seen some of the local natives watching us from afar, but I cannot determine what they want. They do not appear to be threatening us, but they do know we are here. Maybe we will learn more tomorrow."

"But now it is time to hear the next chapter in Sam Hardy's life. In this chapter we hear about the life of Sam's tribe living along the Oregon coastlands. We hear of the fate of his twin sons, and the direction of the tribe after that. They were influenced by the rising sea levels and fears of invasions along the coast from the south. That is when they decided to move to this Sutherlin site.

"Puter, please say to us the next file, Chap-15," said the ProfSir.

The Puter spoke, "The file says,"

In July 2084 the Reedsport tribe that lived on the Oregon coast at the mouth of the Umpqua River had grown to almost four hundred souls. That included my sub-tribe of forty-eight that arrived from Weed in 2079.

When my tribe reached the Umpqua River to settle, everything indicated that we made a very wise decision to move to Oregon. But our first choice of Winchester Point to build our homes proved to be too exposed to the Pacific Ocean. So my extended family rebuilt our homes and docks three miles upstream near the middle of the bay. That put us near the ocean but inside the protection of the sandbar that formed Winchester Bay, still downstream from the main hamlet of New Reedsport.

The residents of the old town of Reedsport had abandoned the low-lying parts next to the tidal flats after the tsunami of 2077 and moved to the hills above the bay. In addition, mean sea level had risen over a meter since the beginning of the century and now climbed about a foot every ten years. That may not seem like much, but the Pacific coast suffered occasional strong storm surges on top of high tides, and no sane person expected the sea level to go back down.

We did a little farming around the town. The tribe's fields provided a community vegetable garden and some maize for grinding and feeding our livestock. As the population grew, the limited ground space for growing more crops became a significant problem. With few grains, most of our diet consisted of whatever we could catch or drag from the sea: fish, crab, oysters, and seaweed.

The roadbed of the old U.S. 101 highway through town could be used in the immediate area, but further north the bridge at Florence over the Suslaw River had washed away in the tsunami, making travel beyond that point difficult. To the south the road ended on the north side of Coos Bay. Across the bay we could see the remains of a much larger community, but now, even with the large fishing industry, no one grew sufficient crops to support even one tenth of the former population in that area.

Both north and south of our little town several lakes nestled in the sand dunes next to the old road. Some of these became stagnant and emptied during the dry season as the rainwater drained into the sandy soil. The mosquito problem grew, and those insects spread many of our diseases. Several cases looked much like malaria.

Inland and upriver on the Umpqua River from Reedsport the rising tides covered portions of old Highway 38. You traveled by boat for twelve miles upstream to reach Scottsburg before you could find a passable roadway into the interior.

The big sandbar across the mouth of the Umpqua River remained in place and served as a breakwater for the interior cove. The strong sea currents collected the sand from the river and grew the bar in size as the sea level rose. It protected us except for the worst of times, and then a rogue wave could crash over the bar and enter the bay.

The tribe's small fishing fleet of sailboats and sculls worked the cove. Over near the mouth of the river at Winchester Bay, the Weed tribe built a couple of larger sailboats that could venture out into the Pacific Ocean in good weather to fish for larger booty. Our catches improved over time, and we brought in a major supply of salmon and rock cod on a good fishing day.

My group built their homes on a sandy hill above Winchester Bay to be near our docks and boats. The group consisted of those who came with me from Weed, including Marsha and my twin sons.

My boys grew to be strapping young men of eighteen years as 2084 began—very outgoing, sharp as tacks, and ready to tackle any task. They continued to grow until they both reached an inch taller than I, and they inherited my curly red hair and freckles, and of course, our family's characteristic four-inch hairy tail.

By the age of sixty-nine my hair had turned all white. It still grew bushy and curly, but when I kept it trimmed, the white color did look more distinguished. I felt great pride when the three of us walked down the street and drew the attentions of every woman we met.

Marsha had been a godsend to me. Eight years my senior, she had followed me since we found each other in Nevada in 2038. She stood by me through the loss of my two wives, and then helped raise my boys after losing her son in the battles with the savages from southern California. Marsha's red hair turned even whiter than mine, her skin wrinkled a bit more, and she began to walk with a stoop.

Both boys turned nineteen in mid-2084. Jerry became captain of the Whaler's Catch, one of our ocean-going sailboats anchored at Winchester Bay. Though young for his position, his words of council drew close attention at every meeting of the tribe. Everyone respected him and accepted his leadership.

His twin brother, Joey, grew into a wanderlust and always wanted to explore the seashore and inlands. With his problems of seasickness, I knew he would never be a success in a sea-going community. But his vision exceeded that of Jerry. He always thought ahead and asked questions about what and where we should go, what we should be planning.

On the night of his nineteenth birthday in July, he said to me, "Dad, there must be some way to find the best people that are left and band them together. There must be some way to save the important parts of our civilization. I want to find those people and bring them together. With enough good people, we can restore the world to its past glory."

I looked at him and smiled. "Joey, you strive too hard for some things, and besides, you should not want to restore the world to be what it was. You should strive to find a new way to live that makes sense in today's world. You expect too much of others. This world has gone to hell, and there is not much you can do about it."

"I will, Dad. I will."

Two days later he met me in the middle of the street in full view of everyone and told me of his plans. Dressed in his hunting clothes and carrying a full knapsack, he said, "Dad, I am going to the old Interstate 5 road, then down along the Rogue, and maybe even to the Klamath. I will look for people who feel like me and who will help me build a stronger tribe, one that will lift us back up from where we are. Within two months I will bring them back to you, Dad, and you can tell them about how great things used to be and how we can be there again."

I stood silent, wondering what to say to my son. In my heart I felt disconsolate, because I could see him failing in his quest. But I told him, "Joey, go and find those people. Come back, and when you do I will talk with the people you bring. But the future is not with me, it is with you and those you find. Look into yourself to see what must be done. I can only tell you of history, and what failed before. You must find the future in yourself."

"I will be back in two months, I promise. We will talk again."

We hugged each other there on the street, and he turned and walked south along the old Highway 101, up the hill and over the crest.

Two months passed, and Joey's memory lingered as the willow leaves turned brown along the river. I sat with Marsha on the Winchester dock, looking out at the sinking sun as it reddened the strings of clouds in the sky. "What do you think? Will he ever come back, Marsha?"

She reached over and laid her hand on mine. "Sam, you and I learned to live with what we have; that is all we can do. Joey is a strong young man, and maybe he decided to go farther than his original plan. But we cannot do anything about it. It is his life to live, however it works out. You cannot dwell on it. You must be the leader for the rest of us here at Winchester Bay."

That meeting in the street was the last I ever saw of Joey. We waited for the two months, then another four. Fifteen years have now passed, and he never came back. We never heard another word about him. He ceased to exist except in our memories.

"Puter, please stop for a moment," said ProfSir ElderJan.

CosandJo exclaimed, "ProfSir, did Joey just walk away and disappear?"

"CosandJo, that is what Sam tells us in his memoirs. We do not know what happened to his son, but he was gone. Life was hard in those days, and everyone faced a great deal of risk. Someone who went on a solitary journey was searching for trouble."

CosandJo asked, "But Sam had two sons, and his son Jerry could have become the source of our tribe. They both had all the right characteristics."

The ProfSir frowned at CosandJo, "You continue to search for your dreams where there is no suggestion of success. We will continue with the narration. Puter, please continue."

The Puter spoke, "The file says,"

I breathed a sigh and leaned back against the plank backrest. "I know. But I didn't want to lose him. He is my own flesh and blood."

"Remember, I lost Jack and Jill, my own flesh and blood. That is the way of life. It is not always perfect."

I turned my head and looked at her, a woman of eighty now. Her body showed signs of growing frailty.

Looking into my eyes, she said, "Sam, you will soon lose me as well. I am getting old, and I feel it in my bones that there is not much time left. You and I are of the past world, and others must step forward to take over what we leave. Our journey is almost done. So be it."

I turned to watch the sun sink beneath the horizon and thought about dying. I did not realize that I had another sixteen years to go.

"Marsha," I said. "Let's go inside and go to bed." She took my hand, and I led her into our bedroom, a small cubicle in my hovel with a pad on the floor and an old cover of ragged cloth. We lay down together, not as man and wife, but as companions finding a way to keep warm from the damp fog of the Oregon coast.

Two weeks later her prophecy came true, and she passed.

The next summer, one morning early in June, Jerry came running up to my small hovel and yelled, "Dad, there's a sailing ship rounding the point and coming in. It looks official." He turned and ran back toward the harbor.

I scrambled off my pad and stepped into my sandals. I followed him down the slope to the beach. In the distance I saw a two-masted ketch making for the harbor entrance.

"Jerry," I called ahead, "send a runner to Mayor Flatiron. Tell him the Coast Guard is visiting us. He should come quickly."

The sixty-foot ketch made a sharp turn and tacked behind the breakwater we built up on the north entrance to the harbor. The boat looked clean and crisp, and the uniformed sailors onboard looked efficient and meticulous. I walked down to the large dock where I knew they must tie up.

The ketch settled into the berth as if it knew where it belonged. I reckoned the captain of this boat to be an experienced seaman and sailor. Two teams jumped to the dock and lashed the fore and aft lines to the capstans. The Coast Guard formally arrived at Winchester Bay.

For the previous ten years or so we had been out of touch with the rest of the world. Two-way communications had been lost, so when the CG vessel arrived, we did not know what to expect. At least it still flew the NAF flag.

As Mayor Flatiron ran up to the dock, the captain of the ketch appeared at the gangplank and stepped forward. He held out his hand to the both of us.

"I am Captain Jim Webb of the NAF Coast Guard," he said. "I am here on a tour to review the status of all port facilities on the west coast."

We introduced ourselves and immediately found it very comfortable to have someone of authority in our midst. I realized that our years isolated from society had been a trying time.

After a short description of our tribe and its functions, Captain Webb gave us a summary of happenings in the rest of the world.

"The NAF is still the world's superpower, though we lost much capability in the past fifty years. The other players in the world lost more," he explained. "My ship is cruising the west coast of North America to ensure we have no incursions from our foreign neighbors across the Pacific Ocean. There is still concern there will be attempts to migrate to our continent."

"What is happening in our country, like down in California?" I asked.

"The internal authorities are taking care of the situations there. We are concerned with keeping our sea lanes free of intruders," the captain replied.

"But we left California because of the horde violence and mobs. Has the violence stopped yet? Is there any chance to go back?"

Captain Webb shifted in his chair, looking uncomfortable. "Look, I cannot give you an official answer about what is happening there, but I would personally advise against going south. The weather is becoming even more dry and violent, and society fell apart in those areas years ago. Even now the savages are spreading up the coast."

"How does the rest of the world look?" I tried to keep my face from showing any expectation or emotion.

Captain Webb did not succeed. His face looked bleak. "The rest of the world is in an awful mess. Energy supplies are minimal, and whatever resources there are face a hard time reaching anywhere else. We are fighting a losing battle with pirates on the open seas. Most of the people in the world seem to have returned to barbarism. It is awful. Be glad you are isolated from everything. You have a chance to survive."

The Coast Guard estimated the country's population to be about one hundred million at that time and expected it to drop to fifty million by the end of the century. He said warming, flooding, and starvation on the east coast were far worse than on the west coast. The top brass expected all those conditions to worsen even more before they got better, with sea levels reaching three meters above last century and average world temperatures up over seven degrees centigrade.

Mayor Flatiron asked, "When will the NAF return the world to normal? Why won't they do something about all this?"

I remember how the captain looked askance at the Mayor and said, "Mister Mayor, the world tipped over the edge fifty years ago, and this is as normal as it gets." He turned and walked back up the gangplank of his ship. The next morning the ship continued its voyage to the north.

"Puter, please hold again," said ProfSir ElderJan. "I have read some of the records of the NAF and Coast Guard in our university museum. We know that government and its forces remained active for a number of years into the twenty-second century, then the records become more and more sparse as they lost their battles for survival. Communities on the coastlines were the last to go."

SueJu asked, "What was left? There are still people in the south, aren't there?"

"Yes," the ProfSir answered. "We know of the humans who still occupy the dry southlands. They live as primitive natives and have come to be in balance with the meager resources of that land. But they have none of the technologies we have been able to save from the old civilization."

The class sat silent, waiting.

"Puter, please continue."

The Coast Guard supplied us with new maps of the Oregon and Washington coast that detailed the underwater geography. Jerry grew excited as he studied them in detail. "Dad, I know this coast, and I want to take Whaler's Catch out and troll along this undersea ridge the map shows. I think we can catch a lot of salmon and cod there. It just looks right."

"It's your boat to command, and we can always use more salmon and cod." I underestimated the phenomenal energy of my son and his friends.

Soon, his crew of young men began rigging more tackle. They opened packages from the old warehouse up on the hill and took fishhooks and nylon-wire from which they could build trolling lines. They built rigging for three days, using all the leftover hooks and line they could find.

"We will fish for two days and return the evening of the second day," Jerry told me. "That should be enough."

The next morning, in the hour before sunup, the Whaler's Catch headed out to sea pulling a line of five skiffs behind it. Fourteen young men clung to the rigging of the boat or rode in the skiffs. I marveled at the enthusiasm of the crew.

It stayed quiet during the day, and several of us watched the horizon, waiting for some sight of the Whaler's Catch. The next day more watched for the returning boat. As the sun set, I instructed several of the younger people to climb to the top of the hill guarding the bay and light a bonfire to provide a beacon for the boat.

The next morning, the town turned out to look out to the sea, searching for the boat carrying our sons. We saw nothing. The seas calmed, and the tides moved little up and down. It seemed like the world had ground to a halt.

It grew hot that day, with the temperatures reaching into the eighties. The wind remained calm, and that meant little energy existed to bring our boats home.

At about six in the evening the winds freshened, blowing in from the sea. Once again the townspeople climbed to the top of the hills to search for our crew. As the red sun set, cries came from the hill. "There they are!" "I see the boats!" "They're coming in!"

Everyone rushed to the docks and watched as the Whaler's Catch and its convoy of skiffs tacked into the harbor and approached the docks. Cries of joy rang from boat to shore and from shore to boat as the fishermen docked. And the whole town descended on the boat to help bring the ocean's harvest to the land. The haul of the expedition filled every nook and cranny of boat and skiffs with fish. That night we feasted on the biggest fish bake ever.

Those were glorious days. Later that year Jerry and I journeyed to the mouth of the Columbia and upriver to Portland to see how things went in the urban areas to the north. We found that places with an overpopulation suffered from a continuous lack of food. If we could bring our catch to Portland, we could sell everything we brought, but what could they offer that we needed? It turned out we could use their salvage. We could replenish our hooks and lines.

The seas in and around Winchester Bay became more violent. The warming climate caused more violent storms, and during the winter months, those storms slammed into the coast of Oregon with their full fury. Their winds lashed the hills above the bay, and sometimes I felt they must be twice hurricane velocities.

But the ocean could be more dangerous when calm. At times the rare, but always possible, huge rogue waves came in from the Pacific. They approached with stealth, slipping silently through the opening of the river and then rising into a massive wall of water to strike headlong into the base of the hills overlooking the bay.

In 2090 my son Jerry simply found himself in the wrong place at the wrong time. A rogue wave crashed in from the ocean and tore the Winchester Bay dock apart. Jerry sat cleaning the net on the fishing boat late at night, and the mound of water made no sound as it picked up the boat and tossed it across the docks into the center of town. A line wrapped around Jerry's leg, and as the boat tumbled, the line cut through the muscle and tore his leg from its hip socket. Jerry bled to death within seconds.

///////// \\\\\\\\\

CosandJo held up his hand and ElderJan said, "Puter, please hold again."

"ProfSir, Sam says he lost both of his sons," CosandJo exclaimed. "That cannot be. That means he had no descendants and cannot be the source of our roots."

"CosandJo, that is what Sam is telling us. We cannot change the past, and he is telling us what happened. I am sorry, for I know you have wanted so much for this discovery to be of the roots of our tribe. But as I have said in the past, the study of archeology is to learn about the past, not to create a past you want to be."

"But…"

The class sat silent, waiting.

ElderJan said, "Puter, please continue."

Jerry's death brought to a head the feelings of our group. We all felt the mouth of the Umpqua River lay exposed and too dangerous. And we kept hearing rumors of hordes coming up the coast from the south. We needed a place that would be safe and where we could grow food. There must be water, fresh water. In early spring my tribe, now my extended family, decided to break off and move to the interior, to what became this village in Sutherlin where I now live.

I suppose my grief after losing my son Jeremiah in a boating accident accounted for much of my personal reasons for wanting to make the move from New Reedsport to Sutherlin. It should not have happened, and it was not expected.

I told my friends, "The ocean is now too much of an adversary, and we must move to Sutherlin to escape the continuing onslaught of the Pacific and the rising unrest along the coast." I suppose the members of our party let me make up their minds for them.

I remembered my visit as a boy to visit my Great-Grandfather in Sutherlin, and told my tribe of what I saw back then. George and Ralph, my two co-leaders, went ahead to scout it out and find a place where we could stay. They returned to tell us of a number of abandoned trailers that we could use to get started.

So later that year, a group of thirty-five of us rowed up the Umpqua River and then followed the old highway until we turned north on the old I-5 roadway and came to Sutherlin. There, nestled in the hills to the east, we found the remains of an old trailer park with some of the old trailers still there. We never found out why the people who used to live there left, but it seemed perfect for what we wanted. Cooper Creek flowed nearby to supply water for drinking and irrigation, fed by a small reservoir in the hills above the camp. A lot of land could be planted with seed, and there did not appear to be any people left to contest our ownership of the land. We found our new and final home.

"End of file," the Puter said.

"Class, tomorrow will be our last full day of exploration in the Oregon Lands. It is nearly time that we pack everything for the return to our home at the University of Hudson Bay.

"We have been very successful in my opinion and have found several major contributions to our study of the history and science of the civilization that preceded ours."

CosandJo said, "But we have not found the roots of our tribe. That was what I wanted us to accomplish."

ProfSir ElderJan shook his head. "CosandJo, you have become fixated on this search for your roots, but we must look ahead, not behind, to find our future. Knowing our roots does not really help us cope with the problems we face. Yours is a futile search."

"Yes, I suppose I know you are right." CosandJo hung his head. "But I wanted to know where we came from. I wanted to know about our ancestors. It just seemed important to me."

"I understand how you feel, but remember, we must face reality. We must be rational. We must accept our fate if we are to survive."

Looking at the rest of the group, he said, "Class, please complete your searches early so we can begin preparations tomorrow to leave within two days."

Chapter 16: Sutherlin

January 30, 2091

ProfSir ElderJan sat down on the pillow. "Today we shall hear the last of Sam Hardy's memoirs. This chapter tells of the pastoral haven his tribe tried to create in the village of Sutherlin and of his lack of success."

The ProfSir looked over his class. "This part of Sam's story shows how one must live in harmony with nature and the available resources. This is the kind of acceptance of the environment that we must achieve if we are to be part of this planet. We must recognize and understand our limitations."

CosandJo waited, masking his impatience for the reading to start. He was still disconsolate that Sam's sons had been lost, erasing the chances for Sam to be the Old Man.

ProfSir said. "Puter, please speak File Chap-16." He began to turn the crank round and round to rotate the disk under the reader head. The Puter spoke,

I began these memoirs over a year ago and then lost track of the commitment I made. I accomplished nothing in the last three months. It is now

May 15, 2100. I wasted so much time since I wrote that first chapter of my memoirs. Today, I forced myself back on it.

I began having these chest pains. I figured I had only a short time left to live and write everything down, but after I decided to continue writing, the pains went away, so maybe if I work at it, I can finish.

I am not worried today about food, for without Ralph and George to feed, there is enough for my frail body. But I do worry about water. The creek is about to run dry again. The weather turned hot early this week, and the northeast winds are whipping in from the Cascade lava fields.

Let me tell you more about how and why my tribe settled here in the Sutherlin Creek valley, next to the old town.

I served as a co-leader of the New Reedsport tribe on the Oregon coast at the mouth of the Umpqua River for over twelve years. Then there came a time in January 2091 when we received reports of the savage hordes advancing up the coast, and I declared to the council that our tribe should move inland to Sutherlin for our safety.

I expected to turn seventy-six later that year, and I knew from long experience the dangers of the criminals encroaching into our lands from the south. I also knew the danger from the sea that kept rising in the west, which had taken my son. I told the tribe if we stayed in New Reedsport, we could be overcome, but only my sub-tribe believed me.

Everyone knew of the Sutherlin site. It lay in the second larger valley off the Umpqua River upstream from the river's mouth at Reedsport. It is about ninety miles upstream as the river winds back and forth, fifty miles on the pathway following the old road alongside the river.

Records from the 1800s told of the fifteen-mile long valley noted for its expansive fields of blue camas, a major source of food then as now. Camas bulbs make a sweet stew if cooked long enough. As industry spread through Oregon, the camas disappeared from the valley, and some thought it extinct.

Early neo-pioneers brought the plant back from pockets along the Klamath River and reintroduced it into southern Oregon in the twentieth century, and it spread into the Sutherlin Creek valley once again. Elk, deer, and wild cattle grazed along the creeks and thrived on the rich food. We hunted those herds, but found it too far to carry the kill back to New Reedsport.

My sons, cousins, and I had explored the region over the years and knew that the Sutherlin area contained a wealth of salvage. The original town site, abandoned for many years, lay alongside the old I-5 roadway. Solitary settlers in the area said most people died or left during an epidemic twenty years earlier that swept through towns along the I-5 Interstate highway. We could use the lands and old structures in Sutherlin, and no one remained to challenge our claim to the place.

The next year in 2092, when no one else would listen, I commanded my associates, thirty strong, to build rafts to travel up the river. We loaded our collective belongings onto rafts for the trip through the tide waters of the Umpqua, and towed them to the old bridge at Scottsburg. We herded our stock along the old roadbed and around landslides to the shallow ford above Scottsburg and drove them across the river to the other side. Our livestock consisted of two cows, ten pigs, and seven goats. The Reedsport tribe would not let us take any of the horses. We took hutches for the rabbits and chickens. We even tied together a flock of turkeys.

We decided that though the river ran well, the rocks and rapids above the bridge could be too dangerous to continue the journey by boat. After unloading our goods and livestock, we sent the rafts back downriver to our friends in New Reedsport and began our journey overland. For the most part, the remains of the old Highway 38 roadbed offered us a path we could travel with ease with each cow pulling a travois.

ElderJan interrupted. "Sam's group decision was to isolate themselves from the rest of society as protection from roaming savages and diseases. As we heard when his story began, the approach failed in Sutherlin when one man unilaterally decided to let a stranger come in, and the whole tribe paid the price. We must always be wary of unilateral action. The tribe must make important decisions together. Decisions must be made by the team."

The Puter continued.

When the tribe reached Sutherlin, we established ourselves in an old RV trailer park next to Cooper Creek and began to mine its treasures. We made peace with our neighbors in the valley as well as south near Roseburg. They welcomed a technologically advanced group such as ours. A few settlers from further east in the valley came to visit, and offered us advice and food in trade for what we could offer. They showed us camas. These native blue-flowered lily plants that the Indians and original settlers found so important in their diet became an important element in our diet as well.

Our first years at Sutherlin felt like paradise. Plenty of water flowed down the creek, and our plantings sprouted quickly and productively.

The process of mining an old community for its salvage became our primary occupation to survive in this world at the end of the century. Anything and everything of the remains of the old civilization could help us survive. No other source existed for what we found. We searched through the old trailers, and later the houses and businesses in the town, searching for any kind of usable salvage. We collected strips of metal, lengths of piping, wire, and sometimes good pieces of lumber. There would never be another supply for these items. We considered all these things to be treasures.

In particular, George and I searched the remains for old electronics like radios, power supplies, solar power, LEDs, and even wire. Technology to make such things no longer existed, and these items would never be manufactured again. They had become magic and priceless.

To our surprise we found a couple of old computers along with disks and memory sticks in the remains of an old garage workshop. The old desktop models, with exchanges of hardware parts, could be made to run. George remembered enough to get them to work. He astounded everyone. They still function, and I am using one of them now to record my memoirs.

We also searched for the more basic tools, like hoes and hammers and nails. One of our greatest finds proved to be a supply of seeds for planting. Our future diet suddenly expanded tenfold, though we still relied upon the camas harvest for much of our food.

We found one of the old hand-powered shortwave radios, one with multiple bands so you could listen to stations around the world. We wired the radio to our solar cells and battery system, and used the hand crank at night so we could listen when radio signals traveled farthest around the globe.

Since 2065, when a solar flare destroyed all the communications satellites, shortwave radio had provided most of the news we heard from the rest of the world. A few radio stations broadcast pretty regularly. Much of what we heard amounted to opinions, though some of the broadcasts came from the government and reported the status of things and what to do.

One of the regular broadcasts we listened to in the early 2090s was a weekly report from the University at Hudson Bay. The university was established back in 2050 in anticipation of things falling apart. They created a sustainable farming community and developed a biomass fuel supply. They called for anyone with old time knowledge to come join them. The university wanted to preserve as much technology of the old world as they could.

The University at Hudson Bay also did research into new things, including using the information from France on building a working fusion power system. They also built a thorium molten salt reactor, but it had not reached critical mass by the end of the century.

The university became one of our primary sources of information for living a sustainable life, with suggestions for planting, generating energy, and making herbal medicines.

ProfSir stopped the reading, "Class, this is the earliest record that I know of that proves our university existed over a thousand years ago. Even then, our founders tried to save the knowledge of the world's former civilization. We can all be proud of our heritage. Give yourself applause."

The class grunted in applause.

He again rotated the disk in the reader.

Knowledge from the university was invaluable. Over the years our tribe had devoted months searching through any abandoned book libraries they could find along the way, looking for old cures. We found some rare books about what plants and seeds from nature to use for medicines, herbs, and food. In the first part of the century, people copied most of the useful information to the Internet and then tossed the books. In 2065 when the Internet died, the few remaining books became treasures.

Our little settlement beside Cooper Creek grew for a while, reaching forty people in 2095, but then the population started down. It seemed almost like clockwork that from time to time we would lose someone to age or in an accident or to disease. Age we could handle, for many of us were pretty well along in years, but disease and accidents scared most in the tribe, especially the younger ones.

It is now three weeks since I wrote the lines above. Talk about speaking within the earshot of fate. Three weeks ago I stood up, and it like felt something broke inside my gut. Suddenly, I got sick as a dog. That's the problem with being alone. When something goes wrong, there is no one to turn to. Whatever my bug, it left me weak and barely able to move around. I survived on the water in my hut and some maize to chew on. I slept a lot, and finally, I felt like writing again. Next time I may not be so lucky. I better hurry and finish this tale.

I remember seventy-five years ago when you went to a pharmacy or emergency medical room to get a cure for whatever ailed you. You could get supplements to help you think better or pills to cure a headache. They even offered pills to cure things you never knew you had.

But in the last half of the twenty-first century, no one could give us vaccinations, so when a new disease crept in, it affected most everyone. Anyone without a native immunity to the disease suffered most, and most often that meant the majority of those in our village. Some of the diseases descended from the old times. I remember how the medical profession bragged about obliterating those old maladies. But there must have been a supply of old germs left over, because they came back, things like small pox and malaria and tuberculosis. What's worse is that many germs and viruses proved to be more virulent than when they happened the first time. Now they often killed the patient.

Accidents scared us most. With nothing in the way of manufactured medicines to help, we used old remedies like poultices. The fear of accidents affected our birth rate. One couple birthed a baby boy in 2093, but the mother died from an aneurysm during childbirth like my second wife, Claire. The six youngest members of our small tribe—the ones we expected to help our tribe grow—remembered too vividly what happened. We encouraged them, but they either could not or would not conceive children. Our tribe no longer grew; it began to die.

When the tribe arrived in Sutherlin, water quickly became our biggest problem. To this day it still is. Cooper Creek flowed down from the remains of an old reservoir and passed our camp on its way to Sutherlin Creek and the Umpqua River. George checked it all out. "This creek is our only source of water. When it runs dry, we must go miles to get any more."

Cooper Creek is fed by springs up in the hills, above the old reservoir. The dam releases water at a steady rate when water is available. The springs depend on the winter rains. Ever since we came here, it rains less and less each year. It's that blasted Baja Line.

As a kid I first heard of the Baja Line on a TV documentary. A climatologist explained how climate change would warm the Pacific coast. "Weather similar to Mexico's Baja California coast at the turn of the century is moving north at about 125 miles every ten years. The place where the spring and fall weather is in the process of changing from predominantly cool fog to warm and dry we call the Baja Line."

They said the Baja Line reached Long Beach in 2015—the year I was born—when Los Angeles County adopted water rationing big time. The city and its suburbs began to suffer the temperatures and desert conditions typical of the northern Baja California desert in 2000. The Baja Line continued to move up the California coast, and according to the most recent estimate it crossed into Oregon in about 2090. I estimate it to be right over Sutherlin here in 2092, and should reach the mouth of the Columbia River by the end of the century, next year. Imagine the state of Washington looking like Baja California. In hindsight, maybe migration to Alaska would have been better.

During our first year in Sutherlin, the creek went dry for two weeks in August and for longer periods each year after that. We dug holes to reach the water table. We dug five feet the first time. We deepened the hole each year after that until the water table disappeared into the bedrock. In 2094 our waterhole dried up mid-September. We sent a party eight miles west to the Umpqua River to get drinking water. Six of our strongest took everything they could carry that would hold water for the overnight trip and brought back about thirty gallons. We ran out within three days and realized the only way we could survive would be to move the entire tribe to the river until the rains returned.

Knowing the tribe must camp next to water, we gathered everything we could carry and tied it into bundles for the trip. George, our handyman, built a small cart from trash parts he found around the old RV park. It carried our heavier items, like our clay oven. We rigged animals to carry packs of things. Dogs and pigs carried their share, and we herded the chickens and turkeys ahead of us. Everything else we carried in packs on our backs. All those things we could not take we hid, hoping no one would come along and squat in our camp while we were gone. We didn't want a fight.

Many in the tribe considered the trek to the Umpqua like an outing. To an old man like me, it became a painful shuffle and a long day's walk. But if I fell, the unspoken rule of the tribe said to leave me there and go on. Better to save the tribe than take a risk on helping an old man.

Once I reached the river, I actually felt better. The tribe set up our cooking pits and everyone drank their fill of water from upstream. We reserved downstream for swimming and washing. You could find clear, clean water in several places amongst the patches of moss. We dug holes for the toilets high up the bank, far away from our water supply. It was a long walk, but worth the protection.

The river flow slowed, but at least the river current continued and did not become stagnant. We rested and improved our camp alongside the river. A supply of old driftwood provided fuel for an evening campfire, and we reminisced of some of the events that brought us all together. We even enjoyed a sing-along, and I sang some of the really old songs from the past, songs my mother taught me as a kid.

For three weeks we camped beside the river, hoping the weather would cool and the river would not go dry. Then a violent wind and rainstorm blew in. Winds whipped cold and wet around our little camp as we huddled next to the river. Within hours the river became a raging torrent, and we moved up the bank. Water roared beside us for three days before the river dropped back.

The next morning George came running into camp yelling, "There's a run of salmon in the river. Everybody, we've got to catch the salmon." The flood must have cleared the mouth of the river and brought a run of salmon into the river, and we caught as many as we could. Everyone enjoyed a glorious time. They swam and used whatever method they could to trap the salmon and move them toward the bank. Some of those fish weighed thirty pounds or more. Members of the tribe gutted them and spread them in the sun to dry. We had food.

I explained to the younger tribe members that when I was a boy, salmon runs in the rivers had become a thing of the past. My Great-Grandpa told me salmon in the rivers on the Pacific coast disappeared when pollution filled the rivers and the water ran out. But enough salmon survived somewhere, somehow. It amazed me that the salmon runs came back so soon.

The weather on the Umpqua turned good with sun and a lot of warm wind, so we could dry the fish we caught for our winter stores. The run lasted another three weeks. Exhausted, we packed up and returned to our camp in Sutherlin and found the creek flowing well.

When Cooper creek provided the water, we used a pedal pump to lift water up from the stream for drinking and irrigation. You stood on it and stepped up and down, like riding one of the old stationary bikes of decades past. George built the pump when we first arrived. "I saw the plans years ago in an Internet story about how they built pumps for the people in India and Africa," he explained.

Most of the year the dry winds came every day, making it hot much of the time. The drought working its way up from the south kept getting worse. During the occasional soaking storms, we caught every bit of water we could and routed it into the rocks above our garden. During the winter months the weather cooled during the day and temperatures got cold during the night.

We had an adequate supply of food during the spring and early summer, but not bounteous. The tribe planted a garden up against the side of the hill to keep it out of the winds. There we could grow fresh greens and squash. We grew some potatoes and beets. We raised beans and even nurtured a melon vine. Usually, we kept someone up near the garden as a lookout. Birds became our biggest problem, stealing whatever we tried to grow. The occasional deer and rabbit tried to be a problem, but that offered the opportunity to add to our supply of dried meat. During the fall and winter our food supply could get a bit short if we had not been industrious during the summer and stored a supply of dried grain, fruit, and roots.

Whenever we found a run of fish in the river or creek, we caught as many as we could and dried the salmon on a stick in the sun. Dried salmon would last several months unless it got wet. We also learned to like ground acorn flour and some of the other native seeds. Mostly we ate flat cakes made from the grindings of the maize and grain we raised. We cooked the cakes on a flat metal plate over an open fire and they tasted great.

We didn't eat much in the way of protein, except for the salmon. Very little wildlife remained in the area, what with it being so dry most of the time. Once in a while someone would run down a rabbit or a squirrel. With that as the base, we would make a community stew with whatever vegetables, nuts, and roots we could gather together. It provided a nice variation to our diet.

The wind blew most of the time, and it got stronger from year to year. Storms came through—some of them pretty awful, even though we were forty miles direct from the coast. With more and more wind, the weather became hotter and drier each year, but we could still raise food. Our supply of meat dwindled, and we caught fewer rabbits and rarely a deer. Of course, when the salmon ran up the river or creek, we caught as many as we could.

Life in the village became a peaceful life, but one filled with vigilance. The tribe agreed that we should be very careful about whom we let approach our camp and make sure we appeared strong to the world outside. We did not want to let some aggressive neighbor run us over. Since we did not go looking for company, we saw very few visitors.

In 2097 we sent a party back to scout on our original tribe at Reedsport near the mouth of the Umpqua. They returned to say no one remained; the buildings appeared abandoned and falling apart, some still filled with meager belongings. They found a few skeletons, but no real evidence to know if the people of Reedsport simply left or died.

The short wave radio told how a monstrous typhoon struck central Japan last year, bigger than Category 5. That, with the dengue fever outbreaks, destroyed the island country.

Most of what we heard from the few travelers coming north confirmed reports from the short wave radio. The few attempts by society to hold its own in self-sustaining villages became targets of the barbaric tribes that roamed the central parts of California. One by one those self-sustaining villages went off the air, and we heard nothing from them again.

Only the Siskiyou Mountains at the California-Oregon border protected us from the savages to the south. So far they had been enough, but I worried that its protection would not last.

In time, the number of people going north along the old I-5 roadway became less and less. They said everywhere to the south was hell. They warned us to be on our guard. I felt we must be the last civilized people left on the face of the earth.

I worried how correct our decision to seek a sanctuary away from the rest of society and learn to live off the land had been. We succeeded in developing that lifestyle, but one on a path to nowhere. Slowly but surely our tribe was dying off. Why did we bother? I thought that maybe if I took the tribe further north, that could rejuvenate us. At least that plan would give us a goal.

And then the man with the plague made the final decision for us. Our village would die.

I scolded Ralph, "You knew the rules, but you violated them when you took him into your place without telling anyone. Our group agreed a long time ago we would apply strict limits on anyone who tried to join us. Now we're all paying for it, and your wife looks like she may be the first to go. I hope you're sorry."

Reading through some of the old medical books collected over the years, it appeared the stranger suffered something like typhoid. The disease proved contagious as hell—it just took a while to show up. The time of antibiotics had long since passed. We would find no cure or miracle drug to save us.

The first indication of his problem appeared when he complained of a fever. He shook under the covers and sweated like he would melt, then the next day he felt okay. He did not suffer from nausea or vomiting, but he wouldn't eat much. A couple of days later, it happened again, and his diarrhea began. Again he came out of it, but quickly experienced another attack with a terrible headache. His body got hotter and hotter as we all tried to help him. But we had no medicines, no antibiotics. Now people fight diseases on their own.

The next night he sat on the pot shaking and hemorrhaging and losing all his body fluids until he just passed out and died. For all I know, the sickness derived from one of those biological warfare diseases the military worked on years ago, or maybe a super-typhoid created by people overdosing themselves with antibiotics or such.

A few days later, Ralph and I started feeling poorly and showed most of the same symptoms, but we got better after a week. Without any kind of medications the sickness spread through the rest of our group like wildfire.

We finally figured out that it spread by the diarrhea and handling the sick. A person felt good one day and sick the next. George suffered a mild case but recovered. Everyone else hemorrhaged and went into convulsions and died. One couple left walking north on I-5, shaking and sweating with fever. They probably died in the wilderness, or passed the disease on down the line.

We flew a black flag to warn people of our sickness problem, but no one showed up. Those people in the village went from house to house helping those in misery until all of them caught the disease and died. Our tribe lost twenty-five souls within three weeks, leaving Ralph, George, and me. Only three of the tribe survived.

And I told you when I started this story, George died of gangrene, Ralph shot himself, and I have now finished writing my memoirs. It has been a year. I guess it was worth it. Now I have only to live with myself.

Soon I will pass. At eighty-five years, I am the last of my Great-Grandpa's civilization that is left in this middle part of Oregon—all the rest are dead or have become savages. I'm sad, but except for recording these memoirs, there is nothing left to …

Sam's voice stopped mid-sentence. The Puter said, "End of File Chap-16. There are no more files."

"So class, Sam's story has suddenly ended. How much have we learned about Sam Hardy? Has he told us more than we knew about the world during the Great Collapse of civilization? Is he part of our ancestry? SueJan, what do you say?"

The young girl shifted and shrugged, "I believe he must be a relation of the family from which we Neu-humans came. His story of the Collapse is in so much more detail than anything I have ever heard. It tells us so much about what we must do to be sure this does not happen again. The world can never support such a large population as it did."

CarlJu raised his hand, and when recognized said, "The people of the twenty-first century never learned to conserve their resources and use renewable supplies. They wanted to have everything without thinking of the future."

DanJo added, "I read how the minds of the human race at that time could not distinguish reality from what they wanted to be real. Most spent their lives in denial of the problems that faced them."

ProfSir pointed out, "Sam stopped mid-sentence. Why? It is almost as if he died, but then who would have put the disk into the storage box?"

CosandJo looked up, still surprised by the sudden ending of the words from Sam Hardy. He had been immersed in the emotion, feeling the words from the old man telling of his life a thousand years before.

"There must be more to Sam's story. Is there more?" he asked.

"No," said ProfSir, "There are no more files on this disk."

CosandJo's voice sounded stressed and worried as he said, "Sam told us that he lost his two sons, and we know what happened to Sam's tribe in Sutherlin. They all died. They did not send part of their tribe away to become our ancestors. So what we have found here does not matter to us. It cannot be our roots."

ProfSir looked as his disconsolate acolyte. "So it appears. But remember, CosandJo, archeology is not the construction of history the way we want it to be; it is the understanding of the history that actually happened. Your great find of the box of discs is not the end of our search. We must let others listen to Sam's story, and maybe they will provide a clue for where we should search next to find our roots."

CosandJo hung his head, "But why, what is the use?" Tears welled up in his eyes.

The ProfSir scowled, "CosandJo, never give up hope. You are trying to make reality be what you want rather than what it is. You need to carefully review your thought patterns.

Turning to the entire class he said, "It would be good to study the local natives in detail, but our time is running short. Tomorrow we will pack our treasures for the remainder of our journey east alongside the big river until we can turn back toward our homes at the Hudson Bay University." With that, the ProfSir rose to his feet and dismissed the class.

REQUIEM: MAY 20, 2100

CosandJo's assignment was helping ProfSir ElderJan pack the treasures collected by the expedition for the return journey to Hudson Bay University. He made notes of which items went into which travel box.

When he came across the dark green stone box he had found in Sutherlin, he picked it up and wiped the dust from it. It was a beautiful box. Someone told him it was made from malachite. He remembered the excitement when he had found it. He held it again in his hand and turned the lid, exposing the inner cavity.

Inside, he could see three additional disks. The ProfSir had kept the first disk, the one with Sam's story on it, and carried it in his special pouch.

CosandJo turned and looked for the ProfSir to ask what had been found on the other disks, but the ProfSir had left the tent. Then CosandJo spied the Puter on the small table across the enclosure.

CosandJo carried the storage box over to the Puter and Magic Reader. He took the first disk out of the cavity and placed it in the Reader. He turned the plate to spin the disk. After a moment the Puter spoke, "Disk is a blank."

The ProfSir had said the other disks were blank, but CosandJo tried the second disk, and again the Puter said, "Disk is a blank."

He lifted the last disk from the cavity. It looked just like the first two, but his doggedness persevered, and he placed that disk in the Reader and spun it for the Reader to read. After a moment the Puter said, "Scanning first file. Format is Word Doc. Language is Aenglish. Contents can be translated."

CosandJo sat the box next to the Puter and ran yelling from the tent, searching for the ProfSir. "ProfSir, ProfSir." He rushed to his leader, who was placing packages into the small trailer. "I found another disk that has words on it."

ElderJan looked up. "Where did you find another disk?"

"It was in the storage box."

"But those disks were blanks. I checked them myself."

CosandJo breathed deep and sobbed, "But the last one was not blank. It has Word files."

The ProfSir strode into the tent. "Come, we will check this out." He knelt by the Puter and began to rotate the disk in the Magic Reader.

The metallic voice of the Puter once again spoke, "Reading from file named Goodbye on Sam's Disk 2."

Today is May 20, 2100. Three days ago the sound from a crowd of people outside my hovel interrupted the end of my yearlong project of writing my memoirs. I left my computer keyboard to see what was happening. Glory to all, I had visitors: a troop of twenty-five men, women, and children, and the leader of the troop proved to be my very own son, Joseph, who I thought had died long ago. After sixteen years, my prodigal son had returned.

I thought Joey was lost when he went on a scouting trip over to the Rogue River and never returned. But he told me how he slipped and fell into the river, breaking his leg. He floated downstream several miles until a woman from another tribe to the southwest of here rescued him. The girl named Sheila nursed him back to health, and he stayed there to take her as his wife. He sired a family and went on to become the leader of her tribe.

"Father," he said, "things are becoming even worse than anyone ever expected further south. Savages are infiltrating up the coast from California as the climate to the south becomes ever more intolerable and dry and windy.

"I talked with Coast Guard boats that visited the Rogue River, and they told me that conditions are only going to get worse, both in the weather and in the societal breakdown along the Pacific coast. I talked it over with my elders, and they all agreed I should lead the youngsters of the tribe north, and then east to the Hudson Bay country." He explained that they had established radio contact with a group that said a cluster of civilized people live there in northern Canada, and he planned to join them. Joey asked me to go along.

I bowed my head and explained, "But I have grown old and would be a burden."

Joey said, "I will not take no for an answer. My tribe needs your experience, and you will teach our children everything you know."

So tomorrow morning I leave with Joey's tribe on the trip to the north. I expect to finish this last file tonight and record all my writings on DVDs and leave that disk with copies of the web pages I collected over the years in the storage box I found. Maybe someone will come along and find my records. Maybe someone will remember us in the future.

And, by the way, I am a proud grandfather now. Sheila is a lovely and strong wife who has provided Joey with three sons and two daughters, ages five to sixteen. All of them are striking specimens with big, strong frames and flame-colored hair, and they are so intelligent, just like their father. And the genetic traits are there. They all have tails. I am so proud. It is as if Claire and I founded a dynasty of giant redheaded geniuses.

But the credit goes beyond Claire and me. It goes to my Great-Grandfather Hardy. Joey contacted Jill Swanson down in Willow Creek, and she sent along her eighteen-year-old twin daughters to go with Joey to the north. They have tails, too.

So this is goodbye. Maybe I have been wrong in my pessimism and damnation of humanity, and there really is a future for mankind on this planet. At least I have joined a group that is beginning the steps to future recovery. God willing, I will have the chance to watch that future blossom. I pray this band will build a better civilization than what my peers built for the last one.

"End of file," the Puter said. There was silence in the room.

CosandJo asked, "ProfSir, were Sam and Joey really part of our ancestors? Did we really come from here?"

The old man bowed his head, shaking it slowly. "Yes, CosandJo, I believe you were right in the beginning, and we have found our roots, the place from which we came. The names are right, the time is right, the source is right."

He breathed a long sigh and looked up at his nephew, tears in his eyes. "It has been a thousand years, and now we must take this knowledge and build a better world than what was done before."

As CosandJo drew a large J on his palm, he smiled and said, "Maybe I can be like Sam."

www.ingramcontent.com/pod-product-compliance
Lightning Source LLC
Chambersburg PA
CBHW060550260626
47161CB00003B/1129

9 780975 567135